EAST

BILLIONAIRE RANCH
BOOK 3

VANESSA VALE

Cover design: Bridger Media

Graphics: Deposit Photos: designwest; Wander Aguiar Photography

1

EAST

"SO WILL you pretend to have sex with me?"

"Excuse me?" I asked. The bar was loud enough where I thought she'd just asked me to *pretend* to have sex with her. This woman, in a flirty dress, jean jacket, and cowboy boots, was looking up at me with an equal mix of embarrassment and interest.

Even in the dim lighting, I couldn't miss the hot flush to her cheeks. It was costing her to speak with me. She wasn't out on the prowl. She wasn't touching me, leaning and pressing her tits into my arm. Batting fake eyelashes. Offering a BJ. Wanting me to go home with her.

None of that.

She was gorgeous and I didn't miss the way men looked at her. They took in her curvy frame, her shapely legs and tits that would spill over any man's palms.

I got hard getting a good downward glimpse of those full swells.

I leaned down—she was at least six inches shorter—and spoke into her ear so she could hear me over the crowd that Monday night football brought in. I picked up hints of lemon over the tang of beer and hot wings. "You want me to pretend to have sex with you? That's not remotely possible."

I couldn't help the way my mouth turned up in a smile because her request was the most ridiculous thing I'd ever heard. And yet she was refreshing. Natural. *Real.*

She was actually serious. After the shit with Macon over the summer, his wake and the discovery that the asshole who'd made my life hell might not even be my father, I was jaded. Worse than that. Fucked up, for sure. I wasn't used to someone so blatantly open and... guileless.

I grew up in a household of hatred and secrets. Of stoicism and damaged souls. Of threats and deals. Why she'd chosen me, I had no idea.

She closed her eyes for a moment, those red lashes fanning across her cheeks. "Yeah, nevermind. Forget I said anything."

She spun on her heel and the hem of her dress swirled offering me—and every asshole in the place—the hope of seeing what color panties she wore. No luck though since it only rode to mid-thigh, but it still made me wonder.

I hooked her arm. No way was I letting her walk away. "Hold up, doll."

She turned to face me, her chin tipped up again. I didn't let go of my hold. Knowing now that she would bolt like a wild mustang, I needed to work this a little differently.

She huffed and yeah, I was as hard as a rock.

"Explain."

"I'm not an idiot, even though it may seem that way. My roommates are in the booth in the corner... no, don't look," she warned, giving her head a little shake. "It's my birthday and as a present, they think I should get laid. A bathroom quickie or whatever. It's not my thing but if I don't do it, they're going to pick a guy for me."

The idea of this hot little thing lifting her dress for some rando—besides me—made me angry. No fucking way was she or her friends propositioning someone else. Just looking at her I knew she'd never done this before.

"Your friends are making you pick out your own guy, approach him and ask him to fuck you. They aren't working too hard on that present. On top of that it's fucking dangerous," I said.

"I know," she admitted, then sighed. "Seriously, I know. That's why I wasn't going to do it. Just pretend so they'd let it go. Hopefully forever."

"Why me? I'd never hurt you, but how do you know I'm not an asshole or a serial killer?"

She glanced at the bar and bit her lip. "I've been watching you with the bartenders and the waitstaff. They know you and seem relaxed when talking with you. You're known here."

That was because I owned the bar. I was a silent partner since I was too busy at the university for anything more. I didn't handle the day-to-day work of running the place, but if I was going out for a beer, I was getting it here.

"Although close up I have to wonder about that." She pointed to my forehead where a butterfly bandage held the cut together that I got earlier in the ring. "Did you get in a fight or something?"

"Or something," I murmured, touching the spot. It didn't hurt all that much. Same went for my sore ribs, but the other guy was far worse. "You've been watching me?" I asked, getting us away from how I burned off my anger cage fighting to other, more interesting things. This night was getting better by the minute. A win in the ring and now her. I wasn't ugly—besides the busted head—but hell, a stroke to the ego felt good. A stroke of her little hand on something else would be even better.

She glanced away. "I noticed you right away," she admitted. "You're pretty hot and my roommates would totally buy that I'd pick you. I had to make it believable."

It was nice to know that I was considered fuckable.

"I… Like I said, my friends are a little drunk and pushy," she added.

"Sounds like you need new friends," I muttered. "They shouldn't make you do shit like this if you don't want to. Especially on your birthday. Whatever happened to buying you shots or a necklace or something?"

She didn't look or act like she'd done a few rounds of tequila.

She shook her head and her long hair, all curly and wild over her shoulders, made me wonder how it would feel to grip and tug those silky strands while I fucked her. For real.

"They're fine," she replied, waving off the fact that her friends were pretty crappy. "Roommates, actually. I need to stay friendly with them since I can't afford a place without splitting the rent." She glanced around. "This isn't my scene. I don't have much free time, and this isn't the first thing I'd pick to do. Again, they're trying to be nice. I'm pretty introverted and all this noise and crowd pretty much drains my battery."

I understood. As a professor, I had to deal with students and leading classes and small groups and tutor sessions and grant writing, unlike my twin, West, who talked to cows all day.

"If they're really your friends, they'd know all that and take you bowling or to a bookstore or get pizza and watch Netflix."

She shrugged. "Well, I'm here. I know this is a lot to ask, and definitely weird. If you can go with me into the back for a few minutes, let them think we're doing it, then you'd really help me out. They'll get off my back about it and I can just enjoy the rest of the night. You could read a book or something."

A book?

I took her hand. As I did, I glanced over her shoulder toward the back corner. Three women tucked in a booth were watching us. I winked in their direction to let them know I was playing along, then tugged the chick my dick was hard for toward the bathrooms. I weaved around people and ducked into the office, shut the door. Locked it.

Her green eyes watched the action.

"I know the owner," I said, not giving her more details, like the fact that I *was* the owner. I didn't run the place. I was more a silent partner to my friend, Mike, but that wasn't important. "And if I've got you tucked back here, I'm sure as shit not going to read a book."

She bit her plump lip and eyed me. "Thank you for doing this. Like I said, it only needs to be for a few minutes."

I laughed. "Don't insult me, doll. Your friends will never think a fuck with me will take only a few minutes."

She opened her mouth to speak, then shut it, catching on. I didn't miss the interest in her eyes. Maybe that was the only way she'd been fucked before. Too fast to be satisfying.

"How are they going to know we actually went through with it?" I wondered. "I mean, if they're crazy enough to push you to fuck a stranger in a bar, then they're going to want proof."

She looked away, stroked her finger along the edge

of the desk. It was fairly neat, but a stack of invoices and receipts were in the middle.

"You show them my panties."

I groaned. The sound slipped out before I could stop it. I had no fucking idea who this woman was or my luck that she'd chosen me out of a bar full of men. I wasn't sure if I wanted to scold her friends, spank this woman's ass for going along with something stupid, or revel in the moment.

I curled my fingers. "Hand them over, doll."

Her eyes widened and she stared at me for a minute. "You'll do it?"

I didn't say anything, just waited. If she looked lower than my eyes, she'd see how fucking hard I was. My jeans were practically suffocating my dick.

With another pretty blush, she reached under the hem of her green dress—a deep emerald that matched her eyes—and shimmied a scrap of lavender lace down her legs and worked them over her cowboy boots.

She held them out and I crooked my finger again. I waited for her to step close, then took them from her. The little bit of material was warm from her body and a little damp.

Fuck me.

"What's your name?" I asked, tucking a long

tendril of her hair behind her ear. Based on the bright color, I thought it might be hot to the touch.

"Ella."

"Well, Ella, you have two choices." She didn't flinch or panic at the simple touch, so I set my hands on her waist and slid my thumbs back and forth. "We can stand here and stare at each other or we can actually fuck. If you're going to hand over your panties to a stranger on your birthday, you might as well get an orgasm for it. Yeah?"

"But... but—"

I tucked her panties into my shirt pocket because I sure as shit wasn't giving them back, then cupped her chin. Her skin was warm. Silky soft. Her eyes were wide, and I couldn't miss the way her pupils dilated. She was into this. Nervous, but not afraid.

"The door's right there." I tipped my head toward it, keeping my palm on her, gentle and reassuring. And because I liked how she felt. "You can walk out now or any time. This is all your call. But knowing your pussy's wet and bare right now has got me hard and wanting inside you."

She flicked her gaze at the closed door, the one that muffled the sound of the music and the crowd. Mike was on a hunting trip and no one else had a key to his office. We weren't going to be disturbed by some drunk searching for the bathroom.

No way would I expose her to that shit.

"Just this, right here, right now," she said, outlining her boundaries, pointing a finger at me, then herself. "Nothing more, right?" She cocked her head to the side and tucked her hair back as it slid across her face. The red color reminded me of fall and crisp leaves. Maybe I'd been hit in the head harder than I thought for thinking that poetic shit.

But it was true.

I shook my head. "Nothing more."

No strings was fine with me. I didn't do relationships. Hell, I rarely did one-night stands either. I was getting too old for it, although this right here was different. Twenty-eight and picky, that was me. But Ella was gorgeous. Sweet. Curves that went on for miles. Between those lush tits, knowing her pussy was bare and the fact that we'd part ways once we left this office, she was the perfect woman.

If I was looking for one.

"Condom," she said, then took a deep breath.

I grabbed my wallet from my back pocket as I kept my eyes on hers. I had no problem suiting up. I always did. I'd never gone without. Not once. And I always used my own protection, the ones I bought and kept. I had to be careful with getting trapped by a pregnancy and I had no interest in my dick falling off. While I didn't think Ella was likely to catch me up in either, I appreciated a woman who protected herself. I held it up. She snagged it and her hands were on my belt buckle before I put my wallet back.

"Easy, tiger," I murmured, smiling at her sudden eagerness.

Her tongue peeked out as she set about her task, undoing my jeans and pushing them along with my boxers over my hips.

My dick sprang free. I groaned. She gasped.

She stared at it. I watched her. Pre-cum seeped from the slit. It was possible I wasn't going to last minutes after all and she hadn't even touched it ye—

Her little hand gripped the base of the shaft and she began to stroke it.

"Fuck, doll." My hips jerked into her hold.

I wanted to see more of her. A quickie didn't mean fumbling in the dark. I pushed her jean jacket off her shoulders and she helped me, letting it drop to the floor. I went to work the thin straps of her dress off her shoulders and...

"*Fuuuucck.*" I ran my hands through my hair,

stunned by her. Curvy. Soft. Creamy skin that my fingers itched to caress and my mouth wanted to lick and suck.

She wasn't wearing a bra because there was some kind of shelf or support system built in. God bless those technical clothing geniuses because those lush mounds were tipped with pink nipples that were hardening into perfect points while I watched.

Yeah, I couldn't wait to get my mouth on one, so I lowered my head and sucked. Hard.

"Oh!" Her hand stilled on my dick as she arched her back.

I licked and kissed across the valley between her tits and worked the other nipple over until it was glossy and reddened as well.

I lifted my head, studied her blurry green gaze. She was right there with me.

It became a need to get her off. To watch her come. I cupped her and she was dripping wet. A gasp escaped those full lips.

My fingers slid over her slit, parted her. Her clit was hard and when I circled it, her hips bucked. She was swollen and wet and soft and hot and... my dick dripped even more.

"Shh," I soothed, but it didn't make a difference. She was primed and ready to go.

Fuck, yes. With the pad of my thumb, I gently worked her clit as I circled her entrance. Taunting, sure. But it didn't matter.

She came just like that.

HER EYES FLARED WIDE and I saw it all. Saw into her, saw that she needed this, wanted it. The fact that she climaxed so easy from just my fingers, a *stranger,* was a fucking turn on. Because it showed how much she wanted me.

"Turn around and bend over the desk."

Her breathing was ragged. The flush had spread down over her tits, hiding the spray of freckles, but she spun about and did as I said.

"Lift up that dress and show me how wet you are."

Looking over her shoulder, her cheeks were as flushed as her nipples. Slowly, she reached back and tossed the short hem of her dress up and over her ass.

I stilled and stared. I'd never seen anything so fucking hot before. With the green dress scrunched around her waist, she was bare except for her cowboy boots. Her ass was wide and round. Grippable. Spank-able. Her pussy peeked out, all swollen and *very* wet. I could see the hint of her fiery red hair. With her bent over, her tits dangled like ripe fruit. And the way she was looking at me, at my dick, I couldn't wait a second longer.

She'd forgotten about the condom and I took it from her fingers which were pressed into Mike's desk. I ripped it open and slipped it on, all the while wondering if I should lick that pussy before I fucked it.

When she wiggled her hips, I knew I had to get in her. I wasn't going to last. She was too perfect.

I'd never been so hard before. Never been so into a quick fuck. Never been so close to coming and I hadn't done more than suck on her nipples.

Stepping closer, I gripped the base of my dick and slid the latex-covered head through her wetness. She went up on her tiptoes and moaned at the contact.

"Yes, please. God. Yes."

I could feel her scorching heat even through the barrier and her consent went right to my aching balls. She wanted me in her, and now.

Gripping her hip and squeezing that supple flesh, I thrust deep in one go.

Her back arched. She cried out and tossed her head back as she clenched around me like a fist. Like I was too big. Like she was…

"You okay?" I asked through gritted teeth.

She nodded, biting her lip. Her inner walls milked and rippled around me as she wiggled her hips.

It had either been a really long time for her, which I doubted was the case since I put her around twenty-two, or Ella was—or had been—a virgin.

And just like that, I'd made her mine.

"Why didn't you tell me?" I asked, holding myself still deep inside her.

She turned her head, looked at me with those eyes, a mix now of desire and worry. "I've never had sex before, that's all. Tab A in Slot B and all that. It's not a big deal and it's done. I wanted to. With you. I still do, if you'd only move."

I pulled out.

"What? Because I'm a virgin you're not going to—"

I grabbed her hips and spun her around, then lifted her and sat her on the edge of Mike's desk. Yeah, I wasn't going to tell him about what we were doing to his workspace.

I cupped her cheek and made her eyes meet mine.

"Oh, we're doing this. Just a little differently. Lean back."

She set her palms on the desk behind her and I hooked a hand behind her right knee. She'd been wet before, but I checked now with my fingers. Her slick heat coated the tips.

She gasped.

"How much of a virgin are you?" I asked, letting my fingers play while my dick throbbed. I'd get back in her but it was about her right now.

"Meaning?" she countered, one auburn brow arching. She was disheveled and pretty much naked, wild and sprawled on Mike's desk and yet the look she gave me was a cross between *stop fucking around* and *fuck me.*

"Meaning on a scale of one where you've never seen a dick before to a five of you've just never had a dick in you."

"Five."

I nodded. While I was caveman enough to wish I'd been the only man to touch her, I wasn't a hypocrite. She deserved sex of any kind as much as anyone else.

I was ridiculously pleased I was the first one to get inside her, and ridiculously crazy for wanting to be the last. I didn't *do* relationships and now I wanted one with this pussy.

I settled at her entrance again and slid in, this time slower and I was able to watch her face as I did so.

"Okay?" I asked once I was buried deep once again.

"Yes," she breathed, wiggling her hips.

I pulled back, thrust home. Fuck, yes. She was tight. Hot.

And responsive because she cried out, thrust her tits up.

I sucked on one plump tip as I carefully fucked her. Testing what she liked, how she felt.

I shouldn't have worried. She wasn't a romance novel Highlander maiden. She was a little hellcat, wrapping her legs around me and lifting her hips thrust for thrust.

My thumb rubbed small circles around her clit. I wasn't sure if she could come this first time, but I was going to try to get her there. I knew it was less about my prowess and more about her headspace. I was big and her pussy was like a vice. It was my job to please her.

Her eyes flew open, and I grinned. "Like that?"

She nodded and her arms gave way and she settled on her back on the desk. It didn't take long for her eyes to fall closed and breathy sounds to escape her parted lips. One hand cupped her tit and the other landed on top of mine and she moved it over her clit how she liked.

My balls drew up knowing this woman owned her needs. I was just a tool to get her there now.

Watching her come was fucking incredible. I

observed as a flush spread across her pale skin. Her pussy clenched down on me in tight ripples. I didn't stand a chance. While she cried out her release, I thrust deep and unloaded in her, my hand slapping down on the desk.

It was like a freight train of pleasure.

I had no idea how long we took to recover. Eventually, I pulled back and took care of the condom. Ella slid off the desk and pulled up her dress, slipping the straps back over her shoulders. The hem fell back over her thighs. She looked my way with a shy smile, but had a satisfied gleam in her eyes.

“Wanna go back to my place for round two?” I asked. Once wasn’t enough and if she was this wild from her first time, I’d think she’d want more before she called it a night.

She licked her lips, watched as I tucked myself back in my jeans.

“Let me go to the ladies’ room and clean up.”

I nodded as she ducked out of the room, giving me one last glance.

I waited, like an idiot, for ten minutes.

Then I went to the women’s restroom to see if she was okay. Not there.

Then I went out to the main bar area to find her friends. Again, not there.

Then I realized I'd been ghosted.

By a gorgeous woman who gave me her name, her virginity and nothing else.

Except… I reached into my pocket and pulled out her panties. The only proof I had of her existence.

2

ELLA

I SLID INTO MY SEAT, setting my bag on the floor at my feet. The classroom was on the second floor of the math building and held about fifty students. Since it was a lower-level class, one I was taking to fill my math elective, it was full.

The hard plastic prompted me to how sore I was and that prompted me to what I'd done the night before. While I hadn't held onto my virginity for any particular reason, losing it had been a pretty easy decision. Because the guy... whatever his name was, was really, really hot. Buff, broad, sturdy. Sexy. And huge... everywhere.

That was why my pussy ached. It was as if I'd been ripped open. Anyone who said their first time was all rainbows and rose petals had been with a small-dicked guy. Or they'd tossed away their hymen riding horses or using huge dildos. Neither was the case with me and there was no way my body was letting me forget how I'd bent over a desk and been fucked by a stranger. Or spun about and made to come. All over his huge cock.

God, that had been hot. I wasn't one to pick up men. I wasn't one to even approach them. I wasn't shy. I was focused. I had no time for extraneous stuff, including man-induced orgasms. I worked and went to school. Studied. I was killing myself, knowing that it was the only way to being a social worker. To a life where I could rely on myself and be financially independent instead of a responsibility or an after-thought.

Except last night I'd been the farthest thing from an after-thought. That guy had been focused on me. He'd cared enough to change things up when he'd figured out my inexperience. I'd thought I'd have been able to hide it, but being impaled on a baby-arm sized dick was a discomfort I couldn't disguise.

Nor was the orgasm he'd given me after he'd laid me out on the desk.

I stuck out my lower lip and exhaled, fanning my face.

At twenty-two, I couldn't have asked for a better V-card punch. I'd seen him across the bar well before my roommates had pretty much pestered me into approaching him. He'd been the only option, pretty much the only guy I'd noticed. He was big. Football linebacker big. Ate three hamburger combo meals for dinner huge. With his dark hair and strikingly pale eyes, he'd been... amazing. God, my ovaries had perked right up at the sight of all six-plus feet of testosterone. He made a red plaid flannel look good. Damned good.

Even a little cut above his eyebrow made him seem rugged. Maybe even a tad dangerous, because he'd been right. Me picking up a guy wasn't the smartest thing. Still, I'd felt oddly safe with him. Wild, too.

Too bad that I'd never see him again. No, not bad. Good. It was a good thing because if I did, I had a feeling I'd be in trouble all over again. It had been intense, sure. But I'd felt more than attraction. Chemistry, too. A connection, and I didn't mean because his huge dick had been in my vagina. I'd felt... special. Like he was just as into me as I was to him. I didn't do relationships. Flings. Anything boyfriend/girlfriend. I didn't have time. I didn't have the interest in one. I didn't have the DNA or whatever it was that made a woman want a guy in a permanent way. Hell, no guy would want me for long term either.

I was shit at love. Maybe it was the fact that I had no love role models. Being a foster kid, I'd had more "parents" than I ever wanted. Most were nice, but not the cookie-making mom or bike ride-teaching dad I'd longed to have. None were overly affectionate with each other, or any of their kids, biological or foster. Especially not Ron. The one who liked his foster kids —girls—a little too much.

I had no idea how to love, being shuffled from family to family, especially since Ron the Perv painted a disgusting picture. At least he was dead and no one else would deal with his shit. I'd made sure of it when he'd passed out drunk with a cigarette in his hand and set his recliner on fire. I'd gotten out, but hadn't even tried to save Ron. I'd made the choice to let him die.

Until the night before, I had no idea how to fuck. But fucking, no matter how good it was, didn't mean marriage. My three roommates were perfect examples of that. I couldn't keep the string of men who came into our apartment with them straight. It was like having a revolving door for a front entrance.

I flipped the lid on my laptop and powered it on.

The classroom was filling up and everyone dropped into their seats.

I worked full time at the distribution center plus carried a full class load. I got little sleep and little free time. On top of that, I just heard I was accepted for a work/study program which would pay for books and other school dues. It was halfway through the semester so I hadn't expected it, but it was good news.

My roommates rarely saw me. While they worked hard on their classes, they partied hard too. I needed to keep my academic scholarship with good grades and needed to pay the bills with my job. I had no option. No family support. Nothing to fall back on like they did. When Thanksgiving came, they went home to sit at a crowded table with aunts and grandparents. Winter break meant tree trimming and stocking stuffers. I got the apartment to myself and time-and-a-half at the warehouse.

Having sex at the bar had satisfied their fun with me for a while. They'd been drunk enough to assume whatever they wanted as I'd tugged them out of there while the guy had been waiting for me in the office.

I didn't need him showing them my panties. I didn't need to draw out the V-card punch. One and done. While my roommates weren't into relationships right now, they were ultimately hoping to settle down. To find The One.

Ironic that they were the ones who slept around and I hadn't touched a man.

I thought of the guy's words. That real friends didn't dare them to fuck strangers at bars. He was right. I knew it. Sarah, Lynn, and Leah were nice and all, but we were roommates first. Friends second. I needed them to help pay the rent. I didn't need to get manicures together. Or pick up men at bars.

The professor came into the classroom as I grabbed my cell, remembering almost too late to turn off the ringer.

"Hi everyone. I'm sure you're all thinking I'm in the wrong room."

I looked up from fiddling with my phone at the deep voice. Blinked.

Holy shit. I knew that dark hair. Those pale eyes. Those broad shoulders. Thickly veined forearms. What was in his pants.

"I'm Dr. Wainright. As you are probably well aware, Dr. Newburgh is having a baby. Well, baby Claire decided to make a very early arrival last night instead of waiting until December. Both mom and baby are well, but a four-pound human has the department scrambling to fill Dr. Newburgh's classes for the remainder of the semester. You get me."

As he spoke, he set a leather messenger bag on the floor beside the podium, then tucked his hands into his pockets.

There had been a pool on the baby's arrival, but I didn't think anyone picked October. Dr. Newburgh and her OB probably hadn't either.

"The department PA is organizing turned-in work for each of her classes," he continued, his gaze shifting across the room as he spoke. "Once I get your assignments from her, I will work through it all. Please give me some time to catch up."

Students chattered about this update, but all I could think about was *him*. Dr. Wainright. My new stats teacher. The guy who knew me in the Biblical sense.

"For a little fun, we will use the model of a baby's due date and the statistical chances of Dr. Newburgh delivering yesterday instead of the expected date of..."

A student in the front row called out, "December seventeenth."

Dr. Wainwright smiled and my ovaries jumped up and down in recognition. "Right. I'm sure she won't mind being used for stats practice."

The class laughed.

I freaked and dropped my cell on my foot, then it clattered on the wood floor.

I started to sweat. My pulse went through the roof. I was probably having a heart attack. Mr. One Night Stand was the substitute professor of my math elective, and he was staring right at me.

EAST

"I HAVE A BIG FUCKING PROBLEM." I shut my office door behind me, set my bag on my desk. Somehow I'd survived an hour long class doing a complex problem on fixed data versus the flexibility of something like childbirth. Only the math itself kept me from thinking of how Ella had looked when she'd come all over a dick for the first time.

Barely.

"Macon? The shit with North?" West, my brother, asked.

I instantly thought of someone trying to kill North. Of her assistant being Macon's lover. Of the secrets she'd finally revealed to us.

"No. Different problems," I replied.

"We still haven't heard back about the DNA tests," he said. While I was in Bozeman, he was on his ranch, a few miles down the road from the big house, almost two hours away.

"You'd think with a billion dollars we could get a rush on those," I grumbled.

"Okay, so you've got a big fucking problem other than you're cranky like you missed snack time?"

I had, actually. I wasn't used to the extra class. I yanked open my desk drawer and pulled out a protein bar.

"The fight last night didn't help your mood?" he asked.

I bit off a chunk of the peanut butter and chocolate. "It was two nights ago, and I guess I need to beat the shit out of someone else."

I had anger issues. Big ones. I didn't need a shrink to know they'd manifested from living and dealing with Macon as a kid. In high school, I took my anger out using my fists on assholes and bullies because I was over six feet tall and two hundred pounds in tenth grade. No one messed with me, except Macon. In college, I'd started fighting competitively. While I'd gotten a football scholarship, the coach hadn't cared about my extracurricular activities as long as I wasn't too hurt to train or play games.

Now I spent time in the ring doing MMA, boxing, and even underground matches. Fight club style. I was one of the biggest guys to compete. I was quick for my size and had plenty of angst and meanness in my blood. The cage fight the other night had taken the edge off my constant aggression.

It had been worse lately. Macon's death had stirred shit up. West knew all about it, but I tried to hide the extent of my drive from everyone else. For now.

"Fine. Two nights ago. What could go wrong there in the big city?" West's voice was as tame as usual. His sarcasm wasn't.

As for the big city, Bozeman, Montana was far from that. But the Wainright Ranch was on the largest swath of privately owned land in the state, which meant isolation and remoteness. The nearest town had a population of less than ten thousand. My name, along with my three siblings, was on the deed for all of it.

"I had a one-night stand," I admitted, running a hand through my hair. I'd had a semi since I saw Ella in the third row. At first, my mind had gone blank and I'd stared, but I'd pulled my head out of my ass and focused. And stood behind the podium to hide the fact that I'd been inside of one of my students less than twelve hours before.

"Okay." My brother drew out the one word to two long syllables. "If you can't get it up, then that is a problem."

"Fucker. I can get it up," I muttered, then thought of Ella. Of her bent over the desk, skirt tossed up and I got it up, right in my office. Shit, now I was hard as a fucking nail and had to adjust myself in my pants.

"Then what the fuck's your problem?"

West was my twin. We looked nothing alike. Behaved nothing alike. I was pretty chill, but West was the most patient person I'd ever met. Of course, as a rancher he didn't have to deal with people all that much. Cows didn't talk back. Or fail a test. Or disappear on you with your dick out and balls empty.

"She picked me up," I began. "Pretty much triple-dog dared by her roommates to fuck a guy at a bar for her birthday. She wasn't game for it, but asked me to pretend to fuck her."

"Someone asked you to *pretend* fuck?" The way he asked made it sound like he'd never heard anything so crazy before in his life.

I laughed, ran a hand over my face. "I know. That's what I said. I couldn't turn her down. She would've gone to someone else who could have been a total asshole."

"You were a gentleman and agreed."

"Exactly. Until I took her into Mike's office to *pretend.*" West knew Mike and had been to the bar before. He could picture it all, except for how hot Ella was.

"But..."

"But we had sex anyway."

"Then what's the problem? Shit, say you used a condom." He was well aware of being a Wainright and the precautions we had to take against those wanting our money. And *only* our money.

I groaned. "Jesus. Of course I used a condom. You know the deal."

South, West, and I didn't fuck without our own supply of condoms. I didn't want to think about North having sex, but the same applied to her. Except now she did it with Jed Barnett. Again, I didn't want to think of them together, but he was different. He was permanent.

"Then—"

"She was a virgin."

He was quiet for a second. "So?"

"So she left me to get cleaned up and never came back."

"Again, so? If it's a quickie that she was into, even if it was her first time, what's wrong with that? I mean, your first time was quick. I bet you were a two-pump chump with Brittney Mendez."

He wasn't too far off but I wasn't going to tell him about my youthful performance. Instead, I said, "Fucker."

"I don't understand what the problem is."

Yeah, why was I so pissed about being stood up? We'd both gotten what we'd wanted. It had to have been pretty uncomfortable for her because I hadn't gone slow, yet she'd still come.

"You should have seen her. She's fucking gorgeous. Red hair. Curves for miles. Passionate. A tiger when she gets going. Once wasn't enough." I dropped into my desk chair, swiveled it to stare out the window. My view was of campus and the Bridger mountains in the distance. That was a problem in itself. Once was *always* enough for me. Even with Brittney Mendez. I didn't do relationships with women. Or love.

While I'd kept up with my siblings since I was the only one who didn't live on or near the ranch, I was just reconnecting with North, South, and West in ways we never had before. Without Macon fucking with all of us, we were free to be... normal. To hang out and be a real family and it was something we all wanted. We didn't have to tiptoe around Macon and his shit.

But a woman? Short term attraction and ball

emptying were my only requirements. Until now. Frowning, I said, “She ran out and left me with only her panties. It’s like it never happened.”

He laughed. “Did she have little mice and forest creatures scurrying around her?”

“What the hell are you talking about?” I snarled. I hated when he fucked with me. I was trying to be serious and he was talking shit I didn’t even understand.

“Did the clock strike midnight when she ran out? What’s her name?”

“Ella.”

His laugh got deeper and went on longer. “Now you’re fucking with me.”

“Whatever. I’m glad you’re finding this funny,” I muttered over him.

“Let me get this straight. You had fun at the ball with a beautiful woman who left you with nothing but her panties to track her down. And her name is Ella.”

“Right. Except for the ball part. It was at the bar.”

“I guess you’re going to have to put those panties on every woman you meet to see if the panties fit perfectly.”

“Are you insane?”

“Are you stupid?” he countered. “Good thing you’re

a math professor instead of English. Ever heard of Cinderella?"

I pushed back in my chair, set my feet on my windowsill. "Oh shit, that's fucking crazy."

"If you want to see her again, then I'm sure you will. It happened for the prince, and he had his happily ever after."

"I don't want a happily ever after," I snarled. I wanted more of Ella. To find out what got her hot, got her off, then give it to her.

"Then what the hell's the matter?"

"I haven't told you the problem yet."

"There's an *actual* problem? How hard did you get hit the other night?"

"I don't have to go searching for her. I'm covering for a fellow professor on maternity leave. Turns out Ella's now one of my students. Which means I can't touch her."

When West didn't stop laughing this time, I hung up on him.

3

ELLA

I FLED the building as soon as class was over. Not only because I had thirty minutes to get to work, but I couldn't spend another minute eye fucking my professor. How had I never seen him at school before? I'd taken a math class freshman year, but not since. I was a sociology major and spent most of my time in a different building. What were the chances of him being the sub?

Why now? Why the day after I picked him out of a bar and propositioned the pants off him?

Why didn't he do a statistics problem about *that*?

The entire time I'd sorted and loaded boxes and

packages at my job—I worked the swing shift in a shipping warehouse by the airport—I'd expected a call or an email from the university, telling me I'd been kicked out. That I'd been a hussy with a professor which was against the rules.

Was it?

Of course it was. I couldn't sleep my way to an A.

It wasn't against the law. I was well over eighteen and Dr. Wainright couldn't be more than thirty. We were consenting adults, but teacher-student relationships?

I *needed* my scholarship. If I got kicked out, or even reprimanded because of a temporary professor of a math elective and I lost that money, my degree would be gone. All that hard work down the toilet. Everything I longed for... poof. Over.

My fingers shook as I worked and I only hoped I'd focused enough to have loaded the trucks correctly. I'd definitely get fired if things ended up on a flight out of town headed to the wrong city.

That panic had kept me tossing and turning. Expelled from college and fired. It was so easy for both of those things to happen. It was like I was spinning plates and if I let one thing fall...

Was I irrational? Probably. I'd been killing myself to get where I was. Close to graduation, all lined up to transition to the master's program for social work. I was right on track with my dream job. No, it wouldn't make me rich, but I'd be paid. Settled. Helping others through a rough time just like I'd had.

I couldn't derail it now for anything. Not even a man. *Especially* not a man.

No matter how much I wanted, I couldn't skip this class. I needed it for graduation. That meant the next day I slunk in, settled into the back row this time, sweating and losing my shit all the while he—Dr. Wainright—completed another complicated problem about predicting the first snow date of the season. Taking notes was easy. I wrote the shit out of the topic directly off the white board. It was far easier than staring at the man who'd made me orgasm all over his dick.

This morning I'd run into Leah and Lynn, who'd wanted to know all the details about the other night, every naughty one. As I poured some cereal in a bowl, I'd told them it hadn't worked out, that while the guy was hot, I hadn't been able to go through with it. They bought it since I was not only introverted but had no time for extracurricular fun. Telling them I'd actually had a quickie in a bar would have been more surprising.

More importantly, there was no way I could tell

them he was my fill-in professor. I couldn't risk a peep of what went down spreading across campus. Fortunately, they were all in different majors, none of them math. Leah was in Economics, Sarah in Psychology, and Lynn in Spanish. I doubted they ever came in this specific building and if I hadn't seen Dr. Wainright before, then I was sure they hadn't. They hadn't said anything about knowing who he was at the bar. Or any time after, thankfully.

When class was over, I packed my bag like everyone else. Before I could duck out, my name was called. "Miss Taynor."

My heart leapt up into my throat and I turned in the doorway, stepping back to let the other students pass as I looked to *him*.

"I need to speak with you a moment." He was still behind the podium, hands in pockets. Relaxed.

Swallowing hard, I started to shut the door.

"Leave it open, please."

I nodded, then joined him at the front of the room. I worried the strap of my bag and tried to stand still. Tears pricked my eyes, but I willed them back.

He flicked his gaze over my shoulder, then said, "About the other night. Are you o—"

"Am I being kicked out?" I asked, cutting him off. I had to know.

He frowned and studied me. My jeans and university sweatshirt weren't as cute as my outfit from the bar. I was only wearing lip gloss and my hair was pulled back in a ponytail. "What?"

I stared down at the metal trash can beside the podium. I couldn't look him in the eye. Cowardly, yes, but I just couldn't do it.

"I'm twenty-five credits from graduation," I explained. "If I'm kicked out now it'll kill my chances of getting into the grad program. I know I approached you and all, but I *need* this class to stay—"

He shook his head. "You're not kicked out, although I should."

My cheeks heated and I wanted to puke.

I looked him in the eye. He was watching me intently, although I couldn't read his expression. His jaw ticked, but otherwise to anyone passing by in the hallway who looked in, would see two people casually chatting.

"You *should* kick me out? I offered for you to pretend. God, this is why I don't get involved with men. You hold all the power. You could destroy my life all because of some stupid prank, which wasn't even really anything."

My lip was trembling, and I took shallow breaths to try and calm down.

His eyes assessed me, moving over my face. "I meant I should reassign you to a different teacher, but it wasn't my class to begin with and I'm only temporary, finishing off the semester."

Well, fuck.

"Actually, you're the one with all the control here," he continued. He still had the little cut above his brow, but the bandage was gone and it had healed some. "You could complain to the dean, and I'd probably be the one in trouble, at the least reprimanded. I might be in the position of power, but you hold it all."

He pulled his hands from his pockets and moved from the dais to stand before me. There was an obvious space between us where he couldn't span and touch me. He wore tan pants that fit his larger frame all too well. The cotton was taut over his thighs. A pale blue button up matched his eyes and the sleeves were rolled up showing off his forearms and hands he'd used to make me come.

"I need this class to graduate," I whispered.

"We have done nothing wrong," he said. "If it came before the dean, which it won't, she couldn't argue it happened while I was your teacher. We were strangers before the other night and I was randomly chosen to fill in for Dr. Newburgh. It appears you agree with that."

I could only nod.

"No matter what I wish to do with you, the only thing I can be is your teacher, and I don't mean in the art of fucking."

My mouth fell open and my pussy clenched. Had I understood him properly? Should I be taking notes?

"You—"

Yeah, I couldn't get out more than that. I remembered where we were and I glanced over my shoulder. No one was in the room and even the hallway was quiet. We were alone, but not inappropriately so.

"You ditched me," he said.

I hadn't expected explaining myself to him, but here we were. "I only wanted you to pretend."

The corner of his mouth tipped up, the first time I saw any real reaction.

"Neither of us ended up pretending, did we? No way could you fake that orgasm, the way your newly-opened pussy rippled around me."

I gasped, because… wow. He was a dirty talker.

"You can't talk like that," I hissed, not because I didn't like it, but because I did.

"Don't get all prudish on me. Not after how passionate you were. You were safe with me the other night and you're safe with me now. It will be our secret. I have no choice but to remain professional when I want to be anything but."

I blinked, although that didn't make me hear him better. "You… you want… more?"

He ran a hand over his face. "I wanted you to go home with me. Now I shall have to wait."

"Wait?"

"December tenth."

I frowned. "December?"

That was weeks away.

"The day classes end, doll. The day I will no longer be your professor and I can give us both what we want."

4

EAST

What the hell had I told her? I was going to wait? For almost two months? I'd made it four *days* and I was losing my mind. It seemed my balls had started to do the talking for me because seeing Ella up close, having her sit in the same seat in the third row—she'd settled into that spot after one day in the nosebleed section—was too fucking much for me. I had to pretend she wasn't in the class just to keep my dick down and to stay on topic. Yeah, that pretending shit was what got me into this situation in the first place.

After our little post-class chat earlier in the week,

Ella had left, hurrying off she'd said so she wasn't late for work. Since then, she'd come to class and hadn't looked up from her notetaking once.

Even the top of her auburn head was the hottest thing I'd ever seen. I couldn't get her out of my mind. I hadn't called West since I'd hung up on him. All he'd do was laugh some more. If I couldn't release this pent-up need through fucking, I did it through fighting. I spent more time at the gym sparring until I was beyond exhausted. My opponents had more bruises than usual.

There wasn't anything different about her than the other students. She blended in, going casual in jeans and sweaters or sweatshirts. Sneakers or boots. Laptop open. She hadn't answered any questions yet, but I hadn't tossed too many out there. I wasn't the most seasoned of teachers—only joining the math tenure track two years ago—but I had my rhythm and knew everyone needed a few days to warm up, to settle into the groove of a new professor, especially in this situation when I took over late in the semester. Statistics was more topic and problem driven than open discussion. Thankfully, I stared at the white board more than the students.

It was a struggle to glimpse those lush curves I'd

gripped, the long line of her neck when her hair was pulled up in a bun on the top of her head.

I wanted another round with her in Mike's office. No, in my bed. That was impossible. There wasn't an official no-fraternization policy, but it was frowned upon. I'd asked. Casually. Hypothetically.

It was the fact that I had to wait weeks to have her. I was a fucking caveman knowing I was the only guy who'd been with her. I needed her like a drug addict needed another fix. I didn't even dig deep into the *why* of that. All I knew was that this need for her would burn out after we fucked. A few times. A weekend.

Then we could move on. But no. No. I had to have blue balls for the rest of the semester.

What kept me sane was reminding myself I didn't do relationships. I just needed to work her out of my system. She had the most amazing pussy, but it wasn't that powerful.

"Dr. Wainright."

I was sitting in my desk chair, feet up and staring out the window. Again.

I spun around at the voice. Valerie, the department PA, stood in my open office doorway. She'd started working at the university when I'd been in middle school, so I deferred to her expertise on most things administrative. She handled all of the department's professors. Our schedules around classes and office hours. I thought of her as North's Julian, although I doubted she'd sleep with Macon or try to kill anyone like Julian had.

I popped to my feet because Valerie wasn't alone. Besider her was— "Miss Taynor."

Ella held onto her backpack strap in a grip so tight her knuckles were white. Her green eyes met mine... for just a moment, then flicked away.

It was a warm day for October and she had on a green sweater, a jean skirt and those cowboy boots she'd had on that night at the bar. She looked... good enough to bend over my desk and push the denim up around her waist. Spank her ass for being impossible to resist.

Inwardly, I groaned.

I blinked, looked to Valerie and hoped to God she didn't pick up on the fact that I was a total idiot lusting after my student.

"I'm introducing Ella around, although I forgot she's in your stats class," the older woman said. "She's picked up a work/study program here in the Math office. Six hours a week."

I nodded at the right moments, but internally I was rubbing my hands together in glee. I'd be able to consistently see Ella outside of class. Talk with her. Watch her. Get to know her.

Get to know her? Why had I even thought that? The only knowing I wanted to do was if she liked to have her ass played with or if she had a gag reflex.

"Good," I said finally, my voice a little rough. I cleared my throat. "Welcome."

Ella nodded and stepped back and turned to move down the hall and onto the next introduction.

"If she's not busy now, I have some copies to make for that grant proposal," I said to Valerie.

Her salt and pepper eyebrow winged up as I had yet to use any work/study resources in the past. I wasn't a needy professor and I was younger than most of my peers and knew how to use a computer and a printer and social media.

"Great, then you can show her how to use the copier," Valerie said with a smirk.

She thought she was getting the upper hand, pushing the complicated duty of explaining the pass-code access system of the copier onto me. Little did she know she was sanctioning alone time with Ella in a small copy room.

"I'll show you where you can store your bag, Ella," Valerie said, herding her away and toward the department's central room where Valerie's desk was, as well as several other unassigned ones used for tutor times and work/study resources.

I spun on my heel to face the window again and shifted my dick in my jeans, willing it to remain a semi.

Macon. Think of Macon.

Yeah, that worked.

I ran a hand through my hair and took a calming breath. "Get your shit together," I whispered to myself. I had a big fucking problem if this was how I was going to react to having Ella nearby.

Shaking my head, I grabbed the folder out of my desk drawer that held my notes for the grant proposal I'd been working on.

I didn't see Ella in the doorway since I was facing away, but I *felt* her there.

Yeah, I was fucked.

I pasted on a smile. Pretended I wasn't lusting after her, then approached.

"The copy room is down the hall," I directed, keeping my voice neutral and my hands to myself.

She turned and led the way, giving me the opportunity to study her ass in her denim skirt.

I cleared my throat. "This paper is due mid-November for a department grant," I explained as we left the department and went into the main hallway.

"I'm writing it with Dr. Trimbly and Dr. Mankowicz. Most write it up on a shared computer file, but I like to draft out my initial thoughts freehand, especially since this one has some formulas."

I pointed to the copy room, halfway down the hall between Math and Anthropology. The ladies' room was on the left and the water fountain directly across.

Ella opened the door and stopped in front of the huge machine. The door slid closed on its own to muffle the incessant drone of the copier that bothered nearby offices. There was a window in the door, so while our conversation couldn't be overheard, anyone walking by could see us.

I grabbed a pink sticky note from the shelf and found a box of pens. I scribbled down my copier code and handed it to her.

"Use this. You'll be all set," I murmured, done with the orientation. Why Valerie thought more instruction was needed, I had no idea. Maybe it was because I had a PhD in math that I had no issue with numbers.

Finally, *finally* she lifted her head and her eyes met mine.

Yeah, I fucking wanted her.

"I want to touch you," I admitted.

She sucked in a breath at my words. "Professor."

"East," I clarified.

"*Doctor,*" she countered.

I did have a PhD so she wasn't wrong. "You can call me whatever you want, but I still want to put my hands on you again."

She glanced through the glass to the hallway.

I stepped back, leaned against the supply shelf and crossed my arms. No one would suspect our topic of conversation was naughty by looking at us.

"You're my professor."

I cocked my head. "If you weren't in my class, would it be different? Would you let me give you lessons in fucking instead of stats? I bet you'd be an eager student."

The idea of her being an avid—and naked—pupil in all the different ways we could make each other come made my balls ache. My dick was hard, and I had to shift it again in my jeans.

She watched, then licked her lips.

That wasn't helping. At all.

"I told you. I don't do relationships," she reminded.

"Neither do I. You didn't answer my question."

She sighed and I couldn't miss the way her tits rose and stretched her t-shirt taut.

"If I weren't in your class, I'd..." she said, then stalled.

"No relationship," I clarified. "Just more mind-blowing sex with me. Just a guy."

She bit her lip, studied her boots, then lifted her head. "Yes."

My dick may have just spurted pre-cum on my boxers. "Then what's the problem?"

"I *am* in your class and we're in the copy room."

"Was it good for you?" I asked.

Her eyes widened and her cheeks flushed.

"You came. I watched you. Felt your pussy clench around my dick."

"Oh my God," she whispered, glancing at the copy machine.

"Was it?" I prodded.

"Yes!" she hissed, the blush creeping down her neck. I wondered how far it went. She gave a furtive glance toward the hallway.

"Then you've got to want more. Need my big dick opening you up again. Once wasn't enough, was it?"

I had to admit, watching her squirm made me fight a smile. I wasn't sure if it was because she was embarrassed or frustrated. When her nipples poked through her bra and t-shirt, I knew my answer.

"It doesn't matter what I want. We can't do anything about this... need. You have no idea what I've been through, what I'm working toward. I have too much at stake for a *big dick.* I'm not interested in any kind of commitment."

My brain got caught on the fact that she had needs that weren't being met.

"Does sex mean commitment to you?" I wondered eventually.

She shook her head and looked at me as if I was crazy. "No."

"You were a virgin until you met me," I countered.

She frowned. "You make it sound like I was saving myself for *you*. It was an opportunity. Nothing more."

"Fine, then we'll have more opportunities. Nothing more. We'll fuck until we take care of your *need* and we're tired of each other." Like that was going to happen. "Then move on." That wasn't happening either. My hands clenched into fists at the thought of her being with another guy. A student who had no clue how to satisfy her. Who'd blow his load before she even creamed his dick.

But if that was how she wanted it, I'd take it. For now.

She turned and faced the copier. Opened my folder I'd set on top of it and grabbed the sheets of yellow, lined paper and set them face down in the tray. Glancing at the sticky note, she punched in the code. "How many copies?"

"Five." I had no idea how many I needed. I couldn't even think about the grant proposal.

She hit the Start button and the machine got busy.

"Even if I wanted to start something with you." Her head turned and her gaze met mine. "A fling, I couldn't. *We can't.* Besides getting in trouble, classes and studying and work take up all my time."

"Weekends then," I tossed out. I was being ridiculous, getting her to try to agree to something that could only hypothetically happen. Still, I needed to know she was just as... needy as I was.

"I work."

"Evenings."

"I work," she repeated, with emphasis. When I gave her a look that made me doubt she didn't get a chance to eat or sleep, she added, "Seriously. I have classes until two and I have to be at the distribution center directly after. My schedule varies week to week, but I put in forty hours. Plus studying. Math might come easy for you, but it's really hard for me."

She came easy for me, but I wasn't going to say that.

I was a billionaire. I didn't have to work. I could fill a pool with cash and swim in it. The Wainright name was well known in the area—although she didn't seem to know my background—but I lived a low-key life and everyone I worked with didn't make a big deal out of it. Because I didn't. I drove a pickup truck. I owned a house near campus, but it was small and far from fancy. I lived off my teaching salary.

"A full-time job plus school?" I asked.

Her spine went stiff and her eyes narrowed. "Some students have mommy and daddy to pay their tuition and their fancy SUV. I don't have that luxury. I can't fuck up my scholarship, even for you."

I tipped my chin up in respect. "I hated my father. I got a football scholarship for undergrad just so I didn't have to touch a dime of his money."

Her gaze raked over me, took in my size.

"You had a father to hate," she countered.

"Your dad died?" I asked. I might have hated mine—no, he wasn't actually my father—but I could still empathize.

She shrugged. "No clue. None's listed on my birth certificate. My mother loved drugs more than me and I got put into the system when I was two. Heard she OD'ed a few years later."

Shit. No wonder she worked her ass off. She had no support. My protective instincts kicked in. I didn't remember my mom. North did, a little bit since she was two years older, but I didn't miss her specifically. I missed the concept of a mother. Of a parent who gave a shit.

The copier went silent, and she grabbed the collated copies.

I stepped toward her. She retreated until she bumped into the wall to the right of the door. Reaching up, I tucked a curl behind her ear, but she held up the copies between us as a barrier.

She swallowed, but kept her green eyes on mine.

"Just like at the bar, the door's right there. I'm not going to make you do anything you don't want. You stay, we're going to do this."

Her green gaze shifted to it, then back.

"No, not fuck here. I wouldn't do anything to get you in trouble," I added. "To mess with your classes or your work. I'm not an asshole. I'm only a very weak man who knows what he wants."

"More like a little boy who can't have a toy he wants."

"You found out the other night I'm all man. You've got to give me an inch, Ella."

She wasn't running for the door. Thank fuck, because I wasn't sure what I'd do if she bolted. I didn't need commitment. I just needed more of her.

"What exactly do you want?"

"You got needs? I'll take care of them," I

murmured, stepping a touch closer. I couldn't help myself.

A little frown formed in her brow. I ran a finger gently over that crease and smoothed it out.

"You wet for me, doll?" I whispered. I leaned close, set a hand on her waist. Waited.

She gave me the tiniest nod, which went straight to my dick.

"I want those panties," I murmured.

Her green eyes met mine and I watched as her pupils dilated. Hmm...

"Remember, you have the power. I'm going to be hard all day with your panties in my pocket knowing you're bare beneath that skirt."

I took the papers from her and stepped back, leaned against the door so my back was all someone would see from the hallway. Waited.

An internal debate was going on in her head. Should she? Shouldn't she? I'd think she was playing coy, but she'd been a virgin the other night. She probably didn't know what got her hot. What her kinks were. Handing over her panties wasn't all that wild. Tame, in fact. But it was a start. Little did she know she was having her first lesson with me right here, right now.

If this didn't do it for her, I wasn't going to push. I

wanted to know what got her hot because I had a feeling whatever it was, I'd be into it too.

Her tongue flicked out and slid across her bottom lip as she reached beneath her skirt and worked her panties off. Watching her was the hottest fucking thing.

I held out my hand and she set the black cotton in my palm.

"Good girl," I murmured, tucking them in my pocket. The words of praise made her cheeks flush and she glanced away.

Bossy? Hell, yeah. Naughty? Fuck, yes.

"I can't touch you, remember? Until December."

"December," she repeated, her breath coming in little pants. I picked up her lemon scent and had to wonder what kind of shampoo she used.

I nodded, knowing that was too fucking far away. "I don't want to find out you were on the prowl for some asshole at a bar. Like I said, you got needs, I'll see to them. I popped that cherry which means it's mine."

She frowned. "Possessive much?"

"You handed *me* your panties. I make you come," I reminded. I didn't just take. I gave. "You know it. Your pussy knows it. Remember, doll. No strings."

I eyed her lips, then stepped back because while I

wanted to spin her around, press her against the wall and take her hard, it wasn't the time or place.

She skirted around me and out of the room. I remained where I was. Intrigued, pissed and aroused. I'd be in the copy room until my dick went down and that was going to take a while.

The more I learned about Ella, the more I wanted her. And not just for sex.

5

ELLA

"You know he's a Wainright," Candace said as I walked with her down the hallway.

I tugged on my mittens as we went. A cold snap had blown in overnight. Fall was officially here. Changing leaves were long gone, replaced by frosty nights. Snow would be coming soon and would start to stick for the long haul until spring.

"I do know the professor's name," I replied.

Candace rolled her eyes and gave me a grin. She was a sophomore, a math major and also doing work study in the department.

"I mean, he's East Wainright of the billionaire Wainrights."

She pushed open the door to the stairwell and held it for me as we were done for the day.

"Billionaire?" I asked, my mind boggled. He didn't look like one, but I didn't know how he would look different.

Her eyes lit up, pleased she'd shared a juicy tidbit. "Hot and rich. I mean, he's big and crazy strong and... I don't know, he could toss me over his shoulder and carry me off anytime." She practically swooned.

I could agree on the hot part. And big. *Everywhere.* In the two weeks since he'd cornered me in the copy room, we'd only spoken about department things. Even when I wanted to ask about why he had a bruise on his cheek one day and a busted lip another. They seemed to match the cut above his eyebrow that he'd had when we'd first met.

Fortunately, another professor had done it for me. "Lose the fight last night, East?"

Dr. Wainright had grinned and replied. "You should see the other guy."

Which meant he boxed or did martial arts competitively. Which, of course, was totally hot.

Everything about him was hot. Which meant I was in trouble.

So I'd tried to stay focused. Neutral. Unattached. I'd proofed the final grant proposal I'd copied for him and then another one. He'd called on me in class and I'd answered without melting into my chair. We'd remained completely appropriate... except for a rare, heated glance.

Even the panty thing had been insanely hot. Sexy, even. Maybe a little weird too, but I didn't know any different since I had zero sexual experience. For some reason, knowing he'd had my panties tucked in his pocket was thrilling. A secret. Something between us that no one else knew.

He'd asked me if I'd been wet. I was always wet when I saw him. Thought about him, even. And now I found out he was rich. Mega rich.

We started down the stairwell, staying to the right as it was busy with others getting to, and leaving class.

"His family owns the most private land in Montana," Candace added.

Wow.

"Their place is called Billionaire Ranch," she added, sounding like a TV documentary narrator.

I stopped on one of the risers and she turned to look up at me. Her blonde hair bounced against the pink collar of her coat.

"That's what the place is named?" It was

completely pretentious and nothing like the Dr. Wainright I knew.

"That's what everyone calls it." She sighed, turned and went down the next flight. I followed.

"Can you imagine having that kind of money?" she asked, although I assumed it was rhetorical since she didn't wait for me to answer. "He must love math a hell of a lot if he's not jetting off to Mexico or Bora Bora right about now. I mean, it's *math.*"

What would I do with that kind of money? Would I spend all my time on a beach? No, I'd use it to help others. I'd still get my social worker license, which meant I'd get my degree. I couldn't be idle.

Someone held the exterior door open and we stepped out into the cold air. The sun was shining but the wind was fierce.

"Thanks for all your help!" she called, waving over her shoulder and dashing toward the English building for her next class.

I was done for the day, at least at the university. I had a shift in forty-five minutes so I hustled to the parking lot.

I tried to start my car, but it wouldn't. It turned over, but barely.

With my hand on the key in the ignition, I stared

out the windshield at the hood. “No. Not now. Come on.”

I tried again. This time it didn’t even click. Nothing.

Shit. The battery was dead.

There was no bus to the distribution center, and it wasn’t anywhere near the university. I could reach out to a coworker, but I doubted they’d be able to pick me up. Not to be on time.

A rap on the driver’s window had me jumping in my seat.

There was Dr. Wainright—I refused to call him East—leaning his forearm on the roof and looking at me, a small smile turning up his full lips.

“Need some help?”

I rolled down the window. The car was so old that it didn’t have power windows. “I think the battery’s dead.”

He stood, glanced around.

“I could give you a jump, but you’re facing the wrong way.”

I was nose first in a spot and there was a row of bushes in a mulched bed that lined the entire length of this side of the lot. He couldn’t pull up in front of me to get his cables to reach.

I flopped back onto the head rest and closed my eyes, inwardly groaning.

"Got to get to work?" he asked.

My eyes popped open, and I stared at him. "How did you know?"

His gaze raked down my body. "You wear jeans and sneakers on days you work."

Long pants were required and sneakers saved my feet after standing for my entire shift.

"And you said you work the swing shift." He glanced at his watch. "That's not too far off."

He'd listened. Paid attention. Noticed.

I wasn't sure if that was sweet or creepy.

"I do, although today I'm working half-shift, covering for someone. I'll… I guess I'll call a cab." That would eat into my budget, but I couldn't be late. While I'd worked there for two years, to the distribution center I was a worker, easily replaceable.

"I'll give you a ride. Grab your things."

I blinked, then glanced around. Campus was never quiet. There were people about, but no one was paying us any attention. Of course if he bent me over the hood of my car like he had the desk in the bar's office, I was sure people would notice.

Still… "I'm not sure—"

A slow smile turned up the corner of his mouth. "It's just a ride, doll."

That endearment. I hadn't heard that in a while in that deep rumble of his.

I didn't have a choice. It was an innocent ride, nothing more.

I grabbed my bag, my keys and rolled the window up. He held out his hand after I shut the door behind me.

"Give me your keys and I'll get your car looked after."

I was surprised by his words and I was sure it showed on my face, because he said, "You need it fixed, right?"

I couldn't do anything but nod, set my keys with the pineapple keychain in his palm and said, "Thanks. Just the battery. Don't let them upsell you on anything else."

"Yes, ma'am." He led me to a very big, very fancy pickup and opened the passenger door for me. I climbed in. "Seatbelt," he said, shutting the door and jogging around the hood to climb in beside me.

Candace might have been right about his money status based on his truck. It was black with four doors, all decked out with a lift and running boards. The seats were heated leather, and the interior had every bell and whistle offered. I couldn't imagine East fitting well in my little sedan, so maybe a guy of his size needed a big truck like this.

Either way, I could get used to it.

Classic rock came from the speakers and he pushed a button on the steering wheel that turned it off.

"Where to?"

"UPC Shipping by the airport."

He nodded and got us on the road out of town. The ride was smooth and the seats comfortable.

"How many grad programs are you applying to?" he asked.

I turned my head from looking out the side window. He gave me a quick glance, then eyed the road again.

"How did you know about that?" I wondered.

"You told me your plan. Graduation, then the grad program."

"Oh, um… Well. Only the one here. I can't relocate. I've got my apartment, my job."

"Continuing on in sociology?"

I nodded. "I'm going to get my Master's in social work."

He slowed then stopped at a red light. "You'll make a good one," he said softly.

When my eyes met his, I swallowed. Butterflies went crazy in my stomach. "Oh?" I whispered. "You can tell that by my stats homework?"

He smiled. "You said you were in the foster care system so you have experience with various government agencies first hand."

"I do. I want to work with kids to ensure they're placed in good homes with good people. That there's a system in place to weed out the bad."

I thought of Ron and his meek wife, Cindy, of how life would have been different if they hadn't been allowed to be foster parents. Not just for me, but for the other kids who had come before me. I wasn't the only girl Ron had wanted, I was sure of it. Except none came after me. I made sure of it.

Being dead did that.

"I know stats is just an elective for you, but you're doing well in the class. You solved the latest problems."

He was referencing the work I'd turned in the day before which had been ridiculously hard.

"Barely. And a B- is not doing well, but thanks for being positive. Math doesn't come easily to me, that's for sure. You graded them already?" I asked.

"Yours."

Oh. I had no idea what to say to that. He'd pulled

my assignment out of the pile of over fifty and looked at it? I'd spent over two hours on it, even connecting with the tutor during my work study time. It meant something, his special attention. Either he was a creeper, or he was curious. I wouldn't be in his truck if I thought he was like Ron. I knew when I saw him at the bar there was something different about him. Not just because he was bigger than most men. Hotter. He was actually nice. Thoughtful, too.

Thankfully we were close to the industrial area and I couldn't take the time to tear it all apart.

I pointed to where he should turn. He pulled up in front of the entrance, the company logo emblazoned on the building.

I undid my seatbelt and turned to face him.

His pale eyes met mine. Held. Dipped to my mouth.

He didn't say anything, only watched me.

I swallowed, suddenly nervous. There was something about East Wainright. Something intriguing. Something more than a bar pickup. He was quiet. Controlled when he wanted to be. I'd seen him unleashed. Felt it. I liked him both ways.

Women ogled him, took in his attractiveness and nothing deeper. Maybe his wallet, if they knew his background. I was learning over these few weeks of watching him—and not touching—that he was more. And that made him dangerous.

"Thanks for the ride."

He nodded, his dark hair sliding over his forehead.

"What do you do here?" he said, glancing past me and to the employee entrance. Others on the middle shift were heading inside. One person's hat blew off from a gust and he chased after it. Snow was just starting to fall.

"I sort and box packages."

He studied me, then frowned. It didn't matter what he thought. It paid the bills.

I turned to open the door.

"Doll."

I glanced back at him over my shoulder. "What's your number?" he asked.

I frowned. "Why?"

He glanced out the windshield and looked up at the sky. "The weather's going to turn. This is Montana, but if you get out early, I don't want you waiting around in this."

"They're not going to close early. They can't. Packages are on a schedule."

He frowned, not thrilled with that, as he pulled out his cell. I told him my number and he typed it in. My cell chimed in my bag. He reached out, tucked my hair back. My heart thrummed at the small gesture. I craved his touch. It seemed all the times we'd been near each other and not been able to do anything only ratcheted up my need. It was like cruel foreplay.

"I'll have your car fixed by the time you're done. If I don't hear from you, what time should I pick you up?" he asked.

"Oh. You don't have to—"

He tugged my arm, pulling me toward him. His lips settled on mine. I gasped and he took advantage and his tongue plunged, found mine. I resisted, for a moment, then sunk into the kiss. It was hot and decadent, potent. My fingers tangled in his hair.

It lasted a second, maybe two. Maybe a minute. When he released me, I licked my lips, blinked.

"Fuck, what you do to me."

"I thought you said we couldn't touch."

"I'm weak around you," he admitted.

I couldn't help but laugh. "You're the biggest and strongest man I know."

"You hold the power," he said, repeating words he'd said before.

"That might be true, but I'm the one whose panties got taken," I grumbled, then squirmed on the seat.

He growled. "Don't remind me."

"We shouldn't be kissing." I said the words even

though I didn't agree with them. His lips were soft and warm and perfect.

"We should," he countered. "We definitely should. We're nowhere near campus and… fuck, doll. You're impossible to resist."

So was he. We were breathing hard and I was sure he could hear my heart pounding.

"What time are you done?"

"Seven."

He kissed me once more, then practically pushed me out of the truck. As I walked into the warehouse, it felt like he wasn't waiting until December any longer. The fact that I didn't seem to care made me panic.

6

EAST

"WHAT?" I snapped, when I grabbed my cell and answered my brother's call. I was horny and frustrated and didn't want to talk to him right now. I wanted to toss Ella over my shoulder and drag her back to my truck, take her home with me and sink balls deep into her. For the entire weekend.

"What the fuck's your problem?" West asked.

I used my blinker and waited at a stop sign for a car to pass. With the strong winds, snow was blowing sideways. It skimmed off the roads, for now.

I was shifting on the seat, trying to get comfortable, which was impossible since my dick was so hard it had a zipper print in it. I had Ella's taste on my tongue. She'd melted into me, been right there with me in that kiss. In wanting more. Fuck!

"I want Ella." There. I admitted it. Words weren't needed when all I had to do was look at my lap. I hadn't used my hand so much for relief since I was fifteen when I was blowing my load any chance I got.

"Cinderella?"

I gritted my teeth. "Will you stop calling her that stupid-ass name?"

"Fine, you want her. Have her."

"I can't." I ran a hand over my face, regripped the steering wheel.

"Because she's in your class," he said. I wasn't sure if it was to get confirmation on the reason or reminding me why my balls were fucking blue.

"That, yes. But also because... shit, you have to see her and you'd understand. She's fucking gorgeous."

"You fuck her again? That the problem? Because I can't think why it would be. She's just a quickie, right?"

I growled. "Don't disrespect her like that," I snarled.

Except in my mind, I had about fifty ways I wanted to disrespect the hell out of her.

"I want her. Seriously want her. Long haul."

"Okay. You and North have it bad."

North was in love with Jed Barnett. They were a permanent thing. Only a few months ago he'd come to Macon's wake and it had been love at first sight. And a total clusterfuck since he'd been undercover FBI at the time investigating her. It was a good fucking thing, too since it turned out her assistant, Julian, had wanted her dead since he'd been Macon's lover.

Now Jed was ex-FBI and heading up security at Wainright Holdings, the family company which North was CEO. After all the shit she shared with us over whiskey and skeet shooting, she needed a guy like Jed to run herd, because she worked herself too fucking hard. She also needed the love and support he gave her, which was unconditional and intense.

I pulled onto the highway. "Know where I'm going right now? A big box store to buy a car battery. Then I'm going to put it in her POS car, then pick her up at work."

"Yeah, you have it bad. I'd say you're pussy whipped."

"Will you be serious for one fucking minute?" I shouted.

"I am serious. You want her for the long haul, have Jed look into her. Ensure she's legit and not after the money."

With his law enforcement connections and the

Wainright family's cash, Jed could get anything we wanted on anyone. West was right. I had to know everything about Ella Taynor and why I was quickly becoming obsessed. Why I was trying really fucking hard to wait out the rest of the semester to get my hands on her again. Because I needed solid reasons why I shouldn't even think about her, let alone buy her a new car battery and volunteer for carpool.

"I should. She picked me up at a bar, so it's possible I was targeted."

She was a virgin though. She couldn't fake that. It wasn't like she'd done the same thing before.

"I think my dick is what's doing the thinking these days," I continued. "Except I don't *do* long haul so why does it matter? Why am I even saying shit like that?"

"You can do a serious relationship. A forever one. You're not broken. Maybe you just haven't found the right woman before now. And it's possible to find one who isn't a gold-digger."

"You're not helping," I countered. "I need an excuse to dislike her, because I'm sure as shit not finding one."

The temptation was there to use my connections to get background info on Ella, except it felt wrong. While I didn't want anything real, I also wanted to get to know her on my own. The *real* way. No information packet telling me who her first grade teacher was and how long she had braces.

"Which is fucking scary because she shouldn't be interested in me," I continued. "People think the Wainrights are a catch, when we're far from it. If people knew the truth... about Macon, about us? She should be running the other way instead of handing me her fucking panties."

"Actually, that's why I called," he replied.

I rubbed my eye with my free hand. "About her panties?"

"Jesus, no."

"I'm guessing it's not good. Just tell me."

"DNA is back. We're not Macon's."

A chill ran through me and a weird smile settled on my lips. Relief. It was a heady feeling, knowing the fucker didn't make us.

"That's not good news?"

"South is," he added.

I almost drove off the highway, but when I hit the rumble strip, I corrected. "What?"

"You, me, and North share the same father, who isn't Macon. South's his kid."

I took the exit and pulled into the huge parking lot for the megastore. I found a spot and killed the engine.

Sat in silence and stared out the window at the blowing snow.

"Is he okay?" Obviously West and I had the same father since we were twins. That was a given we didn't need DNA testing to validate. But all four of us assumed we'd collectively be Macon's or not. All or nothing.

We were wrong. Somehow South, and only South, was Macon's kid. We all had anger issues. Mountains of problems years of therapy couldn't fix. North had Jed to vent to and I was thankful for that. She'd been the closest to Macon, stuck in that fucking house with him. Working with him day in and day out. We'd thought to leave all that shit behind when we put him in the ground.

South couldn't. Not now.

"I'll see him tonight," West said. "Guys' night. We're meeting Matty and Duggar."

I tried to process all this. "He hated us because we weren't his." I meant Macon.

"Probably."

"But South *was* his. Fuck, you remember how Macon used to ride his ass because he wanted to be an artist."

"Yeah."

"He wasn't any kinder to his own kid than us."

When Macon had learned I wanted to teach, specifically math, he'd gone ape shit. It didn't matter that I was exceptional with numbers. Got a perfect math score on my SATs. Could do crazy problems without a calculator.

I'd put his cruel words on a fucking mental shelf and got my PhD anyway. Just as South went to art school and became an incredible sculptor.

"Maybe he didn't know," he suggested, although there was no way any of us could get the answer. Mom had been dead for over twenty years. Macon hadn't told us when he was alive and took it to the grave. "Maybe Macon thought all of us were proof Mom stepped out on him."

The familiar anger rose up like a tsunami. The need to pummel someone with my fists was powerful. "This is fucking bullshit. All of it. I'm just like him."

"You are nothing like Macon," he countered.

"I fight to burn off this anger. Let me tell you, I feel it right now." For South. For all four of us living through Macon's hell growing up. And for what? He'd been gay. He hadn't been interested in women, in Mom, yet he'd married her. Carried on with men. "If he had an issue with Mom having an affair, then he's one to fucking talk."

"I hear you. I'm right there with you."

"Except you don't want to beat the shit out of someone."

"I do. Oh, I fucking do," he replied.

"But you won't. And I will. Tonight." I watched people coming and going from the store. Women with small children tucked into the shopping carts. An elderly couple with their arms interlocked, shuffling slowly toward the entrance.

"It's fight night. I'm calling Callie to tell her I'm in," I said, referring to the wife of the event organizer. He was the face of their business, but the forty-something woman ran the show. She might not fight in the ring, but she could bust some balls if needed. "I'm going. I… I need to burn off some steam about Ella, but now with South, fuck."

"Why are you so dead set against seeing where things go with your Disney princess?"

I thought of Ella walking into work. "She's far from a princess. She works two jobs to make ends meet. She's got roommates who don't give a shit about her."

While it was because of them that I'd met Ella in the first place, I wasn't sure if I could ever like them for putting her in danger by approaching a stranger at a bar. To have sex. She could have been raped.

I gripped the steering wheel, tried to strangle it.

"I think they're called evil stepsisters in the fairy tale."

I rolled my eyes, not that he could see. That stupid fucking story, except for the fact that West was actually right.

"She doesn't do relationships either," I said. "She made that very clear. Except—"

I pulled her panties from my pocket, the ones I'd been carrying since the day she gave them to me in the copy room. The simple black cotton was farthest thing from lingerie, yet I wanted to grip my dick and pump cum all over it.

She wouldn't have given me her underwear if she wasn't interested. She'd been nervous about it, not because of the play between us, but because she'd done it on campus where we could have been caught. She'd said yes to sex, but in December. After she was no longer my student.

She was petrified I'd get her kicked out of school. That I'd derail her plans. She was one focused woman and nothing, not even me and my dick, were going to sway her. It made me respect her even more. She sure as shit had more control than me.

"Our family is fucked up. I take out my anger in a ring using my fists."

"In a ring. With rules. You think you'd hit her?"

The idea of hitting a woman made me sick. "Hell, no."

"Then you're not like Macon."

"Look, I gotta go. Thanks for telling me about the DNA tests. Keep an eye on South."

"Will do."

I set the cell in the center console as I stared out the window which was now fogging from the cold. Ella made me feel. Aroused. Possessive. Protective. She deserved better than me and my fucked up past. I wouldn't hurt her, but I was big. Aggressive. I *could* hurt her. I might not have Macon's blood in my veins, but I'd been conditioned by him. Raised to cower, to fear. But when I grew bigger than him, I learned my size was what protected me.

So I focused on that. Began to fight. To win. To survive.

That wasn't what Ella needed. A survivor. She needed coddling. Protection. Hugs and puppies. Unicorns and fucking rainbows.

I sure as shit couldn't give her that. But I could replace her car battery and pick her up from work. I had to spend the next few hours trying to figure out how to keep my hands off her.

Because the more I touched her, the more it felt like I couldn't let her go.

And that was a big fucking problem.

7

ELLA

When I came out of work at seven, East was there, just as he'd said. Yes, East. I'd started to think of him as that instead of Dr. Wainright because I was learning who he was. The kiss earlier had definitely made us more familiar. Even though it was snowing, he was leaning against his truck. Without a coat. Of course, if I were his size, I probably wouldn't need one either.

He walked toward me as I approached.

"Good shift?" he asked, taking my bag off my shoulder.

I wasn't sure why he did it, but I didn't say

anything. Chivalry? I wasn't all too familiar with the concept.

"It was fine." It was work. There wasn't anything to say about sorting and packing boxes. My feet ached, but that wasn't new. I'd only worked a half shift though, so it was still early.

"Your battery's been replaced, and your car starts fine now." He opened the passenger for me and I climbed in, but he kept a hand on my elbow to help. The interior was warm and cozy.

When he climbed in beside me, I thanked him and pulled my wallet from my bag, hoping I had enough cash to reimburse him. "If you tell me how much it was, I can—"

"Don't worry about it."

He pulled out of the lot and onto the main road. It was fully dark and the snow was still falling. A dusting covered the grass.

"I pay my way," I countered. He might be Mr. Moneybags, but that didn't mean I accepted charity.

"I know you do," he said, keeping his eyes on the wet road. "It's just a battery. I should've bought you a new car because that one needs a lot of work."

I bristled at his tone because that piece of shit car got me from point A to point B just like his fancy truck did. Sure, it didn't have heated seats or power anything, but it worked and was mine.

"Listen—" I began, but he cut me off.

"I'm not trying to start a fight with you, doll. Just say thank you."

I frowned, but knew I wasn't going to win. It was generous of him. Perhaps the expense didn't seem like much to him, but he had put in the time to get one and replace it. And to be my chauffeur.

"Thank you," I murmured, suddenly feeling petty.

He blinkered and pulled into a burger place and got in line for the drive thru. "I bet you're hungry."

I couldn't argue because my stomach growled at the scent that came in through the heater of greasy French fries. When he lifted an eyebrow and waited, I told him what I'd like and he put in our order. He handed me the bags and the drinks, which I set in the cup holders in the complex center console, as he pulled into a parking spot.

Only the building's lights brightened the interior cab.

"Thanks again," I said, pulling out a burger and handing him one.

We ate for a bit, but I felt the need to fill the silence. I doubted I'd have another chance like this where I had him all to myself and I wanted to know about him.

"So, math?" It sounded stupid, but I didn't want to ask him if he collected other women's panties.

He took a sip of his soda. "Yeah. I have a thing for numbers."

That didn't explain all that much. "Big and brainy," I murmured.

The corner of his mouth kicked up. "That's me."

"Didn't you want to go into the family business or something? I'd think a numbers man would come in handy."

He studied me for a moment, took a bite of his burger. "Ah, you heard about me."

I blushed, but I doubted he could see it. Thankfully.

"Word gets around," I told him, crinkling the wrapper in my fingers.

"My sister runs Wainright Holdings. My brothers and I have nothing to do with it. South's a sculptor and West is a rancher."

Their names were interesting, and I wasn't going to comment as I was sure they'd gotten the questions often enough. Based on his size, I doubted he ever got teased.

"What about you? You're serious about becoming a social worker."

I nodded, nibbled on a fry. "I am."

"How come?"

"I told you I grew up in foster care. While some homes were good, some weren't. Same went for the social workers." I glossed over the hot mess of my childhood because I didn't really want to talk about it, and I didn't think East wanted to know the details. It was one thing to want to fuck me, it was another to know how I ticked.

"It's really important to me that kids have someone to talk to. That actually listens and acts if things get bad."

The fancy screen on his dashboard came to life and a ring came from the speakers. He tapped the display.

"Hello," he said.

"I heard you're coming to see me tonight."

A woman's voice came through clearly and I tensed. It was husky and held a hint of humor.

East grabbed his cell from the console, jabbed the screen and put it to his ear. He made it blatantly obvious he didn't want me hearing the conversation.

Suddenly, I wasn't hungry, but I had nothing else

to do but eat. I didn't want to stare at him. He owed me nothing. *I* owed *him.*

"Yeah. Like last time. Sure. Yeah, can't wait."

I ate my fries as he talked, forcing them down with a swig of my soda.

He paused, ran a hand over his neck and flicked a glance my way. Even in the darkness, I could see the tension overcoming him. Feel it in the truck's huge cab. "I'll be there. Soon."

He hung up, dropped the cell. Next, he balled up his trash and stuffed it in a bag. Pulling out of the spot, he drove toward campus. "I've got to drop you off."

I didn't need to be a genius in math to put two and two together. He was meeting up with this woman. Tonight. *Soon.*

He had to get rid of me. Which, it seemed he already had. I might have given him my virginity, but I'd approached him. I'd asked. He'd even pointed toward the door as a way out. Same went in the copy room. I'd given him my consent... and my panties both times.

Sure, he'd said he wanted to have sex with me in December, but it was still October. I had no hold over him. But he'd said my orgasms were his to give. Did he say that because he knew I got wet for him anytime I saw him? Or thought of him?

It wasn't his fault he was big and gorgeous and exceptionally skilled at sex.

Still, I was hurt. Angry.

I could have dealt with the battery on my own and he wouldn't have to wait a second to get to his other woman.

"Plans tonight?" I asked, choking out the words.

He glanced at me, his jaw clenched. "Yeah, doll. Nothing to worry about."

"Oh?" I asked, trying to give him a chance to share more. To get him to tell me the woman was his dentist and he had a late appointment to have a cavity filled.

He stopped at a red light just off campus.

"You should be good to go with your car."

I only nodded as he drove the rest of the way to the lot.

"If you have any other issues, let me know. I don't like the idea of you driving if it's unsafe."

Right. He didn't like it. As if I cared what he thought.

I pushed open the door, the cold air pouring in. It made me realize how posh his truck was. I'd be climbing into my freezing car. If it started. God, I hoped it would. The only way this could get any worse was if it didn't start and then East and his chivalry would have to help some more.

"I've been driving this unsafe car for years. You not liking it isn't my problem. I've got enough of my own."

I dropped to my feet on the pavement.

"Ella," East called.

I grabbed my bag off the floor. "Thanks again for your help." I meant it. He'd really saved me in a pinch. But I knew where I stood. Just another in a long line of women. I had to wonder the size of the panty collection he had from all the women who literally handed them over.

He was that fucking good. Oh, I'd fallen for it.

I shut the door on his truck before he could say anything else. I climbed into my car, just as icy cold as I expected, and it started right up.

I sighed in relief.

With my car running, he pulled away, off to meet his next conquest.

Shit. I wanted to know where he was going. I wanted to see what she looked like. If I compared, which was stupid because of course I didn't. I was a broke college student. East Wainright was a PhD billionaire with Friday night plans all lined up.

I had no Friday night plans. I was going to go home and make some macaroni and cheese and finish a paper. My roommates would already be out. The taillights brightened when he braked at the street. The blinker went on.

I pulled out of my spot and followed him. Yeah, it was stupid. I had to know. I might've been a virgin, but I wasn't clueless about men. We'd been playing a game these last few weeks. I'd started it. I was also going to end it. On my terms. With my panties on.

8

EAST

THE FAMILIAR POTENT anger coursed through my veins along with the adrenaline as I taped up my hands. It was a heady mix that I craved. The need to hit. Punch. Kick. To give an outlet to all the anger and hatred I had for Macon Wainright. For a decade, I'd tried to beat out the evilness inside me because I had his blood. That the cruelty he'd dished out in hefty portions I could unleash in the ring.

Tonight was different. Tonight I knew definitively that I had no blood tie to the man. That it wasn't his DNA that made me this way. There had to be some kind of scientific study, a nurture versus nature comparison that could be done on me.

I slapped my palm against my knuckles, pressing the tape into place.

The idea made me think of Ella and her sociology work. She wanted to be a social worker. Would become one if she kept at her goal. I'd make a great thesis paper for her. How a fucked up childhood forged a fucked up adult.

I dropped the tape into my bag and paced the back corner of the warehouse and grabbed my sparring gloves. I'd seen her face when Callie had called. Listened as she ate her food only knowing half the conversation. I didn't tell her I was fighting tonight. I couldn't. I'd scare the shit out of her with my brutality. I led a double life. The mild-mannered professor by day, the brutal MMA fighter at night. People knew I fought, but at a gym, in tame competitions. Tonight was different. The rules thin at best. I'd never hurt her. *Never.* I could tell that I had by omission alone.

I wanted it all with her, but in moments like this, sitting alone in a fucking warehouse, it was a reminder that I couldn't give her everything in return.

I didn't have it in me. No love to give. I had no idea how it felt, how to act. What to give to make someone else happy. That made me even more riled. Ella was tucked away in her apartment, probably studying, while I was here. She was too fucking good for me.

The crowd cheered and hollered. Whistled and booed at the fight that was taking place. Rex and Callie had bought this run-down building halfway to Butte to run their fights. They'd done little to convert it from its previous life as grain storage. They only built a center ring with fencing around it, the typical octagon for cage fights, and risers that encircled it for spectators. Original bathrooms in the corner were barely cleaned. The low row of grain offices were now changing rooms for fighters.

There was heat, but not much. The hundred or so bodies in the building brought the temperature up.

I didn't care about any of it. I wasn't here for hot cocoa and bedtime stories. I was here for the next match. The fight Callie had scheduled special. With my size, it was hard to find heavyweight opponents, but they were always a draw. The smaller guys were scrappier and had skill and finesse in their moves, but I had power and anger fueling every strike, jab, kick, and choke.

There was a purse, a prize for winning, which I collected each time I fought. I didn't need it though, or want it, donating the cash to a local youth program.

Rex, with his unlit cigar stub wedged between his

teeth, signaled me from across the floor. I cut over to him in gym shorts and rubber slides on my feet. I held out my hands, palms up so he could tie the glove's laces.

"You look ready to kill."

The smirk on his face indicated he didn't give a shit about my mood or offering any way to fix it besides a ring and an opponent. I didn't say anything. We weren't friendly. He offered me an outlet and I gave him huge profits from the entry fees and under-the-table gambling.

I towered over him and he had to tip his head back to meet my gaze.

"Make him tap, but if you break your toy, you can't play with him again."

I looked toward the ring. My opponent was there, hopping from foot to foot. I'd never seen this guy before, but he was probably my weight, but more compact. A few inches shorter. He looked like a tank.

I wasn't afraid. I was never afraid when I got in the ring. Because I knew that whatever was dished out during the rounds, was nothing compared to what I'd endured with Macon.

Rex slapped me on the ass as I headed toward the cage. I left my slides at the bottom of the steps and climbed into the ring. The crowd was a blur around me. It was all white noise. My focus was on my opponent. And finishing him.

ELLA

I WAS INSANE. Definitely.

First, I'd followed East twenty miles out of town to a cinder block warehouse that had seen better days. If my car broke down, no one would know where I was, stuck on the side of the road. Not that anyone would be out looking. My roommates probably wouldn't worry about me until Monday when their drinking and partying had to be replaced with classes.

Second, there was a banner by the front door that read FIGHT NIGHT 8PM. Fight night.

Cars filled the dirt lot, meaning people were inside. I shouldn't go inside, but I was. East was in there–his truck stood out parked a few rows down–and I had to know why he was taking a woman here. I wasn't much on dating, but even I knew this wasn't romantic. It screamed shady and dangerous.

East was a big boy and could take care of himself. Me? Not so much.

Still, I had to go in. Two couples walked past and I pulled up my big girl panties and climbed from my car. I followed closely behind them, figuring being near two other women would make it safer for me. One of them turned, glanced my way when she heard my footsteps. I gave her a little wave. She didn't seem to care one way or the other about me. By the time I reached the door, I was glad to pay the entry fee solely to get out of the cold.

Once through the doors, I blinked, taking it all in. I'd seen MMA fights on TV. Flashy lights, loud music, scantily clad ring girls. This was *not* that. There had to be a hundred people watching. Mostly men. Maybe all men except for me and the two women who I was slowly following as I looked around. Then stared.

East was in the ring with another huge guy. Circling, weaving, hands up. The rowdy crowd cheered. I dashed after the couples and stuck close to them, settling in a second row seat right at the edge of the long bench.

East swung out with his left hand, striking the side of his opponent's head. He followed it up with an impressive kick to the torso. I winced as the crowd cheered. Why was he doing this? It wasn't like he needed the prize money. I now knew the source of the cut he'd had on his head when we'd first met and the other damage I'd seen since.

The guy folded, but didn't go down from that strike. I'd have been snapped in half. East took that crumple to attack, punching and pushing the guy into the metal fencing. There, they struck at each other's bodies, but nothing too hard since there wasn't much room.

A bell rang and a ref–in jeans and a black hoodie–separated them.

The fighters went to opposite sides of the cage and someone on the other side squirted water into their mouths through the openings.

I wasn't paying the opponent any attention. I only had eyes for East. And his body that was on full display. His shorts hit him just above his knees, but there were slits on the side that hinted at his very sturdy thighs. His legs were thick and corded, just like the rest of him. His six pack abs had six pack abs. And that V thingie showed as the shorts rode low. God, he was incredible, his skin glistening with sweat, the angles and plains in highlight and shadow from the harsh overhead lights.

When we'd had sex at the bar, he'd been fully clothed, only the front of his jeans open and tugged down enough for his dick to be out. I'd been neglected, missing of all that muscly real estate, that was for sure.

I glanced around looking for Callie, the woman he was meeting. Why would he bring her here?

"Ella?"

I turned at my name being called.

Holy. Fucking. Shit. Working his way past the other spectators in my row was a guy I never thought I'd see again. Never wanted to.

Blood rushed in my ears and my heart beat so hard I was lightheaded.

"RJ," I said, my lips numb.

RJ, or Ron Junior, was older than the last time I saw him. Five years ago after the house fire. The one where his father had died. Where I'd *left* him to burn to death.

RJ Silvers wore jeans and a canvas jacket. A ball cap. Leather boots. He blended right in with the crowd. I'd never have noticed him if he hadn't come over.

Now, with him sliding onto the bench beside me, I picked up every little thing about him I remembered. The dark hair. Darker eyes. He had whiskers now, not the patchy fuzz from when he was eighteen. A year older, he'd watched out for me. Or that was what he'd said he'd done. Watched out? No. *Watched?* Hell, yes.

I'd been equally creeped out between father and son. While Ron Senior had been blatant in his interest, handsy and verbally repulsive, Ron Junior had been the complete opposite. A lurker. Perhaps even a stalker. Following me to school. Around the house.

I'd been creeped out then, but thankful when I'd been reassigned to a different foster family. It had been the one and only time in all the years in the system where I'd looked forward to relocating. After that night their house burned, I'd never seen RJ again.

Until now.

"It's been years. I never figured I'd see you again. And here of all places. God, you're as beautiful as I remembered."

He was twenty-three now. Older. He was looking at me with man's eyes. With a new depth of understanding that a little time in a bar's back office with East had made me familiar with.

I licked my lips and he watched the action. Even though East had been a complete stranger, I'd liked his hands on me. It had felt good. Arousing and... safe.

Sitting next to RJ scared the shit out of me because he looked just like his father. Except RJ had done nothing wrong five years ago when his family's house burned down. I had.

"Yeah," I murmured, trying to be as vague as possible. The less I talked, maybe he'd go away.

"What are you doing here?" His dark gaze was fixed on me.

"I'm... with a friend," I lied, trying to look anywhere but him.

"Do you live near here? You're a long way from Burnside."

That was the neighborhood where we'd lived.

The bell clanged again and the fight was back on, which allowed me to turn away, but every particle of my being was focused on RJ. God, why had I come? If I hadn't been petty and angry at East, jealous... I'd be in my apartment, studying. RJ would never have seen me. I'd been so stupid!

The crowd went wild with a solid hit from East. I was on the edge of my seat, my fingers clenched together, trying to move as far away from RJ as possible.

"Don't worry about the fighters," RJ said, slinging his arm around my shoulder.

I popped to my feet, shrugging off his arm. Someone coming down the steps bumped into me because of my abrupt action and he tumbled the last few risers to the concrete floor. RJ grabbed me and kept me from following.

The guy was drunk enough to pop up and give a bow along with a sloppy grin, but people threw empty plastic cups at him for being a dumbass and for being a distraction. Drops of beer landed on me and I wiped them off my face with my coat sleeve.

When I looked up, East wasn't focused on his opponent, or the guy I'd tripped, but me. His eyes widened in blatant surprise at seeing me here and then narrowed. His jaw clenched at RJ's hand on my arm.

Oh shit. I ripped out of RJ's hold once again and moved to the middle of the steps. If others wanted down, they'd have to go around.

Shit. East was in the middle of a cage fight and he only saw me.

Then he got punched in the face. Hard. His head rocked to the side and spittle flew from around his mouthguard. I gasped and put my hand over my mouth. What had I done?

He hadn't been blocking or defending himself because I'd distracted him.

I winced and ignored the people around me checking me out since I'd messed with the fight, RJ in particular. The crowd shouted and clapped. Booed East for not having his head in the game–literally–and cheered for the opponent.

East blinked and finally put his focus where it belonged. On the stupid fight. He wiggled his jaw and turned to face his opponent again. There was an energy shift in him. It was subtle, but I noticed it. I noticed everything about him. Anger and intent practically radiated off him. East threw a combination of punches and kicks that pushed the other guy back, then knocked him to the ground. East, even at his size, pounced and… finished him.

"Let's get out of here. I'll take care of you," RJ said, but I shook my head, otherwise ignoring him.

From where I stood, I couldn't tell what East was doing, but he was sprawled on top of the other guy and I saw a hand smack at the mat. The ref flung his arms out and East hopped to his feet.

He circled once, as if prowling over his victim, then strode to the fence, opened it and…

Oh shit.

He stormed over to me, his gaze never leaving mine. Any spectators in his way cleared fast because he wasn't stopping for anything. Everyone watched as he came up the risers and stopped right in front of me. He was so big, so broad and looming. I'd never seen him so intense, even in the cage. I tilted my chin back and stared. He turned and glared at RJ, whose hand was still gripping my upper arm.

With the same speed as he had in the cage, he shoved RJ, knocking him back onto the risers, falling against the legs of the people in the higher row. "Keep your hands off her," he practically snarled.

I panicked because East couldn't know about RJ, about my past. I might not have killed Ron, but I hadn't saved him either.

He turned to me, RJ done with. He bent down and tossed me over his shoulder.

"East!" I cried, my hands settling on his... gulp, tree trunk thighs.

The crowd cheered and clapped to my complete mortification. I couldn't see anything except East's taut, shorts covered ass as he carried me away. I had no idea where he was taking me, but instead of being worried, I was thankful. With every step we took, I got farther from RJ and my past.

9

EAST

"Do you have a fucking death wish?" I asked after I set Ella back on her feet.

She blinked, took in the changing room, one of the only places with a hint of privacy in this shit hole.

I didn't look away from her as I kicked the door shut with my foot, the crowd noise muffled, but still loud. Rex wouldn't delay the next fight unless someone shot up the place. Maybe not then. He had his eyes squarely on the money.

"I..."

My jaw ached from the punch. It had only landed

because I'd been distracted. By her. By the guy's arm around her shoulder and I'd been able to tell by the look on her face she hadn't liked it

Jesus, she was *here*.

Holy fuck.

The thought of her in the parking lot alone, walking in alone, sitting in the stands all by herself…

I wanted to hit something all over again.

When she didn't do anything more than stutter, I pushed on.

"What the hell are you doing here? This isn't a place for you. Fuck, you could have been hurt or… worse."

I ran a hand over my sweaty hair imagining any one of those assholes in the crowd getting their hands on her. No, one guy'd had his arms wrapped around her.

"Who's the guy you were with?"

Color leached from her cheeks, but she shrugged off my words with an easy answer. "No one. Just a guy who got a little handsy."

Yeah, that only proved my point, which only pissed me off more. "Exactly what I'm talking about! I carried you out of there in front of everyone, and no one stopped me." I pointed at the door. "No one's knocking on the door to check on you. I could be violating you all kinds of ways and no one cares. That's the kind of shit hole this place is."

She turned away.

It was like the fucking Wild Wild West.

I needed to calm down. The post fight adrenaline was rushing through my veins and combining that with Ella in my arms, my dick was hard.

She couldn't miss it. Not in my thin shorts, although she was looking anywhere but at me. Her arms were crossed over her chest and studying a stain in the concrete. It was probably blood. Definitely not mine.

"Ella," I prodded. "Why are you here?"

"You were meeting up with another woman!" she shouted, finally looking at me.

I saw the anger and hurt in her green eyes.

She must have seen the surprise in mine because that was the last fucking thing I thought she'd say.

"What the hell are you talking about?"

"In your truck. The phone call. You left me to meet up with that woman."

I stared, thought about Callie's call from Ella's perspective. "That's why you were pissed when I dropped you off?"

"I'm not to troll for guys but you can make plans with a woman in front of me?" she asked, flinging her hands in the air. "I know we said no relationship or commitment, but I didn't expect you to be such an asshole."

I paused, wiped the back of my hand over my mouth. Considered her words. I wasn't used to this. While we weren't in a relationship–*that* we agreed on–there was something between us. I hadn't ever had to consider a woman's feelings before, even with expectations firmly in place up front. Because I'd never wanted more than once. Never wanted to protect and yeah, possess someone before. I'd never, ever told a woman that her pussy was mine, that her orgasms belonged to me.

Why had I done so with Ella? I had no fucking clue.

I exhaled, tried to chill out. "I'm not sure if I should be pleased at your jealousy, surprised that your anger brought you to such a dangerous place *alone*, or thrilled that you want me enough to even give a shit."

"We're not in a relationship," she snapped. If looks could kill, I'd have tapped out by now.

I arched a brow and took a step toward her. I liked her like this, all riled and... alive.

"Then why are you here? Why are you angry? Why do you care so much?"

So many whys I sounded like a four year old.

"Because I want you. More of what we did at the bar," she admitted.

I liked that answer because finally... finally, I knew she was right there with me.

"Same goes for you," she countered. "Why did you carry me out of there if you don't care?"

I glanced at the closed door, to the crowd and the fight just beyond. "You don't belong here, doll. This isn't your world. None of those assholes should even look at you. They're probably thinking of all the different things they want to do to you."

"I didn't come here for them. I came here for you. Besides, you're the one who dragged me off like a caveman."

"Yeah, and my dick could pound nails right now and it's your fault."

She gasped and her gaze dropped.

"Where's the woman you met here? Have her take care of that." She pointed and circled her finger toward my dick.

It was time to set things straight. I might fuck and forget, but I would never hurt a woman by being callous. I'd never even encountered this problem before. Ella was a first for me too.

"Callie, the woman who called, is one of the organizers of this event. She and her husband run this shit show." I glanced at the water-stained ceiling. "I left her a message earlier and told her I wanted on the roster and she called me back to confirm."

I wasn't telling her about West's call, the reason why I'd put myself on tonight's roster. Ella had learned enough about me already.

"Oh," she whispered.

I stepped closer, taking my life perhaps into my own hands, and tucked her hair back behind her ear. I did it as often as I could because I couldn't help it.

"I have zero interest in the woman," I said. "I might have a hundred pounds on her, but she's ruthless enough to rip my balls off if I even looked at her sideways. Since I don't put my hands on women in anger, I'd have to let her and I like my balls right where they are."

"Then why do you do this?" she asked. The anger was gone from her voice, but the confusion still filled those emerald eyes.

"I fight, doll. This is me. This is what I do."

"Why?"

That was the question West had been asking me

for years. There were other ways to deal with my issues. Counseling, for one. Maybe that worked for him, if he went, but not for me.

"Because I'm fucking broken and this is the only way I can heal."

She laughed, then reached up and gently cupped my cheek. Her eyes roved over my face as if searching for something. "Heal? You've got a split lip and a bruise forming on your jaw."

I wasn't going to tell her they were her fault. Instead, I walked her backward and to the wall, but kept space between us. I wanted her, to strip her of her clothes, press her up against the wall and fuck her until I forgot my own name. To put her on her knees and have her suck me dry.

Not here. Not this place. It was tainted and not just with my fucking nightmares. Every person in this place had shit to deal with and I wasn't letting any of it touch her. Including me.

"Seeing that guy's hands on you isn't helping." I looked her over. Her sneakers, jeans, heavy puffy coat. Any guy with a dick and eyes would know she was gorgeous, even with all of her curves hidden. I might have shown her how to fuck, but she looked sweet and innocent. In this shit hole, Ella walking through that door was like dangling a piece of meat in front of a pack of lions. "Especially knowing it wasn't wanted. I told you no other men. No one else touching you."

Yeah, I sounded like the caveman she accused me of being. Seeing that guy in the crowd touch Ella had pushed me to finish the match faster than any Macon-driven anger.

"I... I want your hands on me," she admitted. Her breathy admission was shy and daring for her.

The words went straight to my balls.

"Except I'm afraid of what would happen if someone found out," she admitted.

The repercussions were all on her. I'd get a slap on the wrist, maybe fired, but I wouldn't go hungry. I wouldn't lose my house. As a man, I'd probably be smacked on the back and given a beer for bagging a hot coed. Ella would be the one who tried to sleep her way to an A.

A total fucking double standard. I'd protect her in this as I would in all things. Like the fucker in the stands or anyone else who put her hands on her but me.

"No one from campus is here," I reassured. "No matter what we do, it's just you and me. I don't flaunt my flings so no one has to know. Nothing's going to happen to you. I'll see to it."

She bit her lip, studied me, then nodded.

Fuck. "I need to be inside you. But I'm not doing it here. Not with another man's sweat on my skin. You're coming home with me."

The fact that she didn't argue or even think about leaving her car behind told me everything I needed to know. Ella was along for the ride... which would be her on my dick.

10

ELLA

I SHOULD DEBATE or at least think twice about this. Being with East. But I couldn't. Like he said, no one from campus knew we were together. Not my roommates. Not anyone else.

Except RJ. I pushed the thought of him aside. He was a problem and one I'd have to deal with. Later. Or hopefully never again. East had made it pretty clear to stay away.

He took my hand and led me through his kitchen, great room, and bedroom and to his bathroom. For a billionaire that Candace described, his house wasn't fancy. Or overly big. It wasn't downtown but closer to the mountains in a neighborhood with huge lots. Set up on a hillside, the view would probably be spectacular during the day. It was a one story rancher that had been updated. Glossy wood floors and trim. Tan walls with paintings, not posters. His furniture was big and overstuffed, as if this was his sanctuary and liked comfort. His bathroom was larger than my bedroom in the apartment I shared. A huge walk-in shower, gleaming tile and beneath my socks, it felt as if the floor was heated.

He reached for the knob and adjusted the temperature as the water cascaded down from a rain head in the ceiling, then turned to me. "I'm not touching you until I get clean." We'd left our shoes in the mudroom, but he pushed the sweats he'd put on before leaving the shady warehouse to the floor. He had nothing on underneath so his dick bobbed toward me. I stared openly as he shucked his sweatshirt, his head covered briefly.

I'd seen his dick at the bar, but only to watch him roll a condom on. The full effect now as it jutted from a nest of dark hair, heavy balls beneath, all between solid thighs... impressive. Instinctually, I knew he was very well endowed, that it actually had fit inside me. That it was going to be bringing me even more pleasure than the first time–hopefully without any discomfort or lingering soreness.

"Like what you see?" he asked.

I flushed, realized I'd been staring a little too long.

He had no modesty, standing big and bare before me. He shouldn't. God, he was the perfect specimen of a man. I felt so small, so... weak beside him.

"Sorry," I murmured, but I wasn't and the turn of my mouth probably gave me away. The steam from the shower was making the room warm.

"You're wearing too many clothes, doll." His hand worked the zipper down on my jacket.

I watched. I never remembered anyone helping me dress or undress before, even as a child.

"I've never showered with anyone," I admitted.

He grinned. "I told you I wouldn't take you with another man's sweat on my skin. I probably stink too. Not sure if I can make it much longer than that."

For some reason, his desperation and need for me made me wet. Made me feel... powerful. Not weak.

My coat fell to the floor at our feet. I took over, pulling my shirt over my head as he climbed beneath the spray and grabbed the soap. With floor to ceiling glass, he scrubbed and washed the fight away while watching me strip.

I wasn't embarrassed. He wouldn't have brought

me here if he didn't like what he saw. Stepping in beside him, I closed the glass door behind me. It fit both of us easily and had a bench seat. Like his truck, I felt spoiled by the understated luxury. I could get used to it. Especially with East enclosed with me.

He pulled me close, his dick nestled between us. One hand tangled in my hair, tugged so I was looking up at him. His body blocked the spray as he kissed me. Hard. I gasped at the intensity of his need, and he took advantage. His tongue plundered. Ravaged. I felt the tile at my back as his leg settled between mine. I was lifted and practically rode his hard thigh.

Unlike the last time, there was nothing between us. No clothes. No one outside the door.

I whimpered as I rolled my hips, my clit rubbing against him.

His hand cupped my breast, thumb brushing over the tip. Then his head dropped and took over.

"Oh!" I cried, my fingers tangling in his wet hair.

The heat of his mouth as it suckled and tugged was incredible. I had no idea it could feel so good. It went right to my clit, the sensations, as if they were magically connected by a string. One pluck at my nipple and I ached to be filled.

His hands roved over my wet skin, as if he had to learn my curves with his calloused palms. He dropped to his knees and his mouth was in line with my breasts. With hands circling behind my back, he pulled me in, almost hugging me so he feasted on one taut tip then the other. Back and forth he went as he stroked my spine, my butt.

He growled, then spun me about so I faced the tile. I put my hands up, my cheek and sensitive nipples grazing the slick surface.

"Fuck, you're gorgeous." With an arm about my waist, he pulled my hips back so my butt was practically in his face. "Oh yeah."

I looked over my shoulder at the heat in his gaze, the smile on his face. "I've been wondering how you taste. Now I get to find out."

Oh. "Oh," I breathed as he put his mouth on me from behind. His tongue licked up my seam as his hands cupped my ass, spreading me so there wasn't anything he didn't see or flick with his tongue.

I knew guys went down on a woman. I knew she liked it. I heard my roommates talk about it all the time, if a guy was good at oral, how skilled his tongue, if he could even find a clit.

Well, East was good. His tongue could get a gold medal in oral olympics. And he found my clit because I begged and pleaded, whimpered and moaned at how amazing it felt. When he slipped a finger into my pussy and did some magical curl, I cried out his name. And when the thumb on his other hand pressed against my–

"Holy fuck, East!" I screamed.

Yeah, I came as I rode his face and tried not to think about how much I liked to be finger fucked in my pussy *and* my ass.

Only when my knees started to give way did East stop, kissing my inner thigh, then standing. His arm hooked around me, palm cupping my breast as he nuzzled my neck.

"Good?" he murmured.

"Cocky much?" I asked, smiling. I looked at him again, this time with a sated, satisfied body.

He stepped back, settled on the seat out of the spray. Steam swirled around us and I was far from cold. With his knees parted, his dick was long and thick, curved toward his rock hard abs. It was a dark ruddy color, a bulging vein pulsing up the length. He gripped the base, stroked it.

"Climb on." He said the words, then closed his eyes and clenched his jaw. "Wait, doll."

He stood, left the shower and opened a drawer on his vanity. Cooler air billowed in as he grabbed a condom, ripped the package open with his teeth before working the latex down his huge length.

He lifted his gaze from what he was doing, eyeing me. "Gotta take care of you, yeah?"

I was reassured to know he had a clearer head than me, that he put my protection before anything else. Except I wasn't sure if he was protecting me, or him. An unexpected pregnancy could be considered entrapment, especially to a man as rich as he was. Or the other way around, him trying to keep me for eighteen years, but I wasn't sure as to why he would. I wasn't even skilled at sex.

Yet when he returned to the shower bench, the glass door silently closing us into our warm cocoon, I couldn't miss the way he looked at me. The way he pulled me onto his lap and carefully lowered me onto him. He was watching me as if this was exactly where he wanted to be. In me. Nowhere else, with no *one* else.

And then he moved, lifted me up by my hips, lowered me down and I stopped thinking.

"Fuck, doll, you're so tight. That okay? You're not still sore?"

My eyes flared wide at the feel of him with me on top. "I'm okay. Just give me a sec."

It didn't hurt, not like the first time in the bar, but he was big. Really big and I felt him opening me up. Stretching me to take all of him. It was so different than being bent over, or pseudo-missionary, if that's what it was sprawled out on a stranger's desk. East bottomed out and there was a different bite of discomfort, just shy of pain.

Yet I was so wet, he moved within me easily. I set my hands on his shoulders and began to move on my own.

"Good girl. Yeah, like that."

My breasts swayed near his face and he leaned forward and licked one.

I had no idea what I was doing, just chasing the pleasure.

"It's so good. I'm... I'm going to come," I breathed, getting a leg workout as I rode his dick. My orgasm was close, but just out of reach.

His hand came between us and he ran a finger over my clit. That was all it took and I cried out. "Professor!"

He groaned and lifted his hips up from the bench, thrusting hard into me. "That's right. I'm your teacher for this. You're gonna be a good student and be fucked all night, aren't you?"

His dirty talk made me come even harder and all I could do was nod. Because right now, I'd never felt like this, and I wanted to, again and again. I had no idea a guy could really talk like that. Not stupid stuff in movies, but what I thought of his words were so naughty, so filthy.

And I liked it, which was a problem, because I also liked him. While I definitely didn't want a relationship and he'd all but said this was a fling, he was different. More because he made me feel things I never even knew were possible. And not just orgasmic bliss.

His hands gripped my hips hard enough I was sure I'd have bruises. He pulled me down, held himself deep as he snarled into my neck, licking and sucking as he came.

Holy shit. I tried to catch my breath as I clung to his muscular shoulders.

Professor Wainright wasn't a stuffy math nerd. He was a sex god.

11

EAST

I'D NEVER BROUGHT a woman back to my house, never considered it. I'd also never imagined I'd sleep with a student. But here I was, carrying two mugs of coffee into my bedroom. One for me and one for the naked coed who'd rocked my world. Again.

It was early, the soft morning light coming through the thin curtains. I didn't like a pitch-black room, so it would be bright in here soon. Ella was asleep on her stomach, her hair fanned around her head on the pillow. I felt like a romantic asshole as I sat on the side.

I was bringing her caffeine instead of kicking her out. Hell, I should have called her a rideshare to get her home after I took her the second time. The *first* time in my bed.

My dick was getting hard again, just thinking about setting the dark brew on the bedside table, tugging the blankets down and settling on top of her. Taking her from behind–like I had that first time when I took her cherry–allowed me to go so deep, my balls slapping against her pussy.

Fuck. I was in trouble because I knew she'd be warm and sleepy, responsive and shit, what a way to wake her.

So I did just that, set the mugs down, grabbed a condom from the table where I'd left a string of them, pushed down my boxers, rolled it on and climbed back in bed.

She stirred as I nudged her legs apart with my knee. "Mmm, morning," she murmured.

Her eyes opened and she smiled at me as I slid my hand up her bare leg.

"I love your ass," I admitted, stroking and squeezing that pert flesh.

"You're a morning person," she said, glancing at me over her shoulder. "I should hate you."

When my hand cupped her pussy from behind, she bent her knee to widen herself up for me.

"But you don't," I replied, finding her wet.

When I slid a finger inside her, she moaned and her eyes fell closed. Her hands reached for the headboard. Why was that so fucking hot?

"But I don't," she whispered, rolling her hips. "East."

I took that as a green light to fuck, hooking my arm about her waist and raising her hips enough to settle at her entrance and slowly push in.

We groaned in unison as I took her at a slow and leisurely pace. I kissed her shoulder, her neck, whispered in her ear as I moved deep inside her.

You're fucking perfect. This pussy was made for me. I'm going to tie those hands to the headboard the next time so I can do whatever I want. This ass, maybe I should fuck it next.

I didn't know how to stop talking about the next time, because the idea of this being the last I was in Ella wasn't going to work for me.

Reaching up, I grabbed one of her hands and guided it down beneath her. "Touch yourself. Come for me."

She'd been a virgin, but I was sure she'd masturbated before. When she worked her clit in small circles, I knew I'd been right. She used a certain number of fingers, a certain circular direction, pace, pressure.

I'd watch her soon, learn how she did it.

The idea of sitting in my reading chair while she was in my bed, naked and open, touching herself made me come. I roared my release as she moaned, her pussy walls clenching and milking me, as if never wanting me to leave.

I finally got up and went to the bathroom to take care of the condom. I brought back a washcloth and cleaned her up, rolling her over onto her back. Only then did she blush.

She must've looked at the bedside clock because she said, "I have to go to work."

I handed her a coffee and she sat up, adjusted the pillows and leaned against the headboard, taking the blanket with her to cover her breasts.

I grabbed my boxers from the floor, slipped them on and sat on the side of the bed. I grabbed my coffee, then tugged the comforter down.

Rolling her eyes, she took a sip. I got to drink my coffee with a gorgeous woman in my bed with her perfect tits on display for me to enjoy, my balls empty, my body sated and relaxed.

"I wasn't sure how you liked it, so I put a little milk in."

"It's good."

"Someone's brought your car from the warehouse," I told her, not going into detail about how I'd paid a guy to do it before dawn. "The keys are under the mat. I hope you don't mind that I got them from your purse."

A woman's handbag wasn't a place for a man. The contents were mysterious and complicated but we'd abandoned her car way out of town where I didn't even want her going in daylight.

"Thanks," she said. "What do you tell people on campus about your fighting? I mean, you had a butterfly bandage on a cut the first time we met."

I looked down at the crisp white sheets, all perfectly tousled. "I belong to an MMA gym. I take classes and fight there. Do some competitions."

"That's what? A front for these underground matches?"

I shrugged. I wasn't sure why I was telling her all this, letting her ask these questions. They were probing and besides my family, no one knew these details. I kept them secret for a reason. Maybe it was because I could look at her plump nipples instead of her face. Maybe it was because she was pretty much a stranger. No, that wasn't fucking true. It was because she was different. She was... Ella and I wanted her to understand the truth, even when I tried to keep it from her.

"You shouldn't have been there last night. Shouldn't have followed me. I should flip you over and spank your ass for that."

A slow smile crept up her face and she hid it behind the mug. "Not sure how much of a punishment that would be."

I growled at the idea of her over my knee. Of her liking it.

"I was there, East. Saw how you were." She leaned forward and cupped my jaw. In the bathroom mirror, I'd seen the bruise from the punch I hadn't blocked when I'd found her in the crowd.

"My mom died when I was little. We–my sister and brothers–grew up with our father. Macon Wainright. He was... an asshole. Mean. I'll spare you the details, but nothing we did was good enough. He died in July."

She didn't say anything, just listened with those green eyes on me as she sipped her coffee. I didn't talk about the money, how most people wondered if everything could be solved with a few million dollars tossed at a problem.

"North, she's two years older, she worked with him at Wainright Holdings. My brothers and I found out she made deals with Macon to let us go to college, to be what we wanted."

"Deals?" she asked, frowning.

I reached out, lifted the blanket up to cover her. I changed my mind, not wanting to taint even the sight of Ella's body with talk of Macon.

"I found out Macon was going to have someone break my leg so I couldn't play football, couldn't get my scholarship for college. All because he thought math was a stupid career."

Ella set her mug down, took mine from my hand and crawled over to me. She wrapped me in her arms from the side, set her chin on my shoulder.

I could feel the usual anger growing, but the heat of Ella's touch, the feel of her naked and supple body pressing against me, soothed it.

"It didn't happen," she murmured, stroking my hair.

I shook my head, her fingers sliding over my scalp. "North agreed to some shit, gave up her happiness for us."

"You said he's dead."

"Yeah, heart attack. In bed with his lover. His *male* lover." I had no idea why I let that slip. None of us had told anyone about the fact that Macon was gay. The truth was a powerful weapon and billions of dollars couldn't stop the destruction it could cause.

"Oh. Wow," she said. "You fight because you're mad? Because of what your sister did?"

I sighed. "I fight because I have his anger and it needed an outlet. I couldn't be like him, hurting and destroying the lives of people around me."

"You think you'd do that? Hurt others?"

"I sure as shit won't have kids. I mean, I don't even know how to be a good parent. How to take care of someone." I shook my head. "I couldn't do that to a baby."

I glanced at her, into those green eyes.

"I can relate. I have no clue how to do that either. I didn't have parents. Just... legal babysitters until I turned eighteen."

Shit. While I'd grown up in hell that looked like a fancy mansion, she'd been all alone. I'd had North, South, and West with me. We'd survived together. The things North had done for us was proof that we'd had someone on our side. That I would always have them.

But Ella didn't have anyone. I shouldn't worry, but I did. I didn't know why I wanted to protect her, to keep her in my bed safe and sated, made no sense.

We fucked. It was amazing. But there could be nothing more.

"Then you can understand why I do it." I sighed, remembering my call with my brother. "Yesterday, after I dropped you off, we got the DNA tests back.

Macon's not our dad. Me and West. And North. But South's his kid."

She frowned. "Weren't you relieved?"

"Why am I so angry then? Why does rage build and force me to let it out with my fists?"

"Because things were out of your control and you can't go back and change it."

I blinked. Her words made sense. Fighting in the cage was controlled. A focused outlet. An opponent who wanted to be there, who probably had similar issues and wanted to let them out on me. None of us could fix that Macon was South's sperm donor. There was nothing I could do about that, no matter how much I hit or kicked or tapped someone out.

Well, fuck.

"Ever consider yoga instead?" she asked.

I couldn't help but laugh, which was probably the point of the question. The idea of me trying to bend into any kind of pose was crazy.

"I can't touch my toes, doll, but if you wear one of those tight little outfits, I might be swayed." I ran a hand down her arm, thankful for her. No matter what West told me, he hadn't gotten through to me the way she just had, and he'd been trying for years. "Although I like you like this even better."

"Naked sex therapy?" she asked, her eyes twinkling. "I could be up for that."

My dick stirred. "So could I."

I realized we were talking about more. About her being in this bed again. She must've caught on to that at the same time because her smile slipped, and she climbed from the bed. "I should go. I need to go back to my apartment, shower and change clothes. Thanks for collecting my car. I'd have had to rush otherwise."

"Will your roommates wonder about where you've been?"

"You mean the walk of shame?" she asked, grabbing her panties and bra from the floor. "They were probably out partying. They don't get up until after noon."

I snagged the panties.

"Oh no. I'm running out." I let her grab them back and watched her slip them on.

"I don't like that fucking term. There is no shame in what we did."

"You're my professor," she reminded me, although I was sure her pussy was sore as she covered it, so she wasn't all that upset. "My roommates might sleep around, but they stick to other students."

"Boys," I said. "You got a man because that's what

your pussy needs. And I'm not grading your work based on your dick sucking."

She stilled as she put her bra on. "I don't think we've gotten to that part of my lessons."

She didn't blush or shrug off my dirty talk. Even as a recent virgin, she was confident in her sexuality, in discovering what made her hot, and it wasn't a fumbling coed. "Oh, doll, we'll get there."

"December."

I wasn't sure if I could wait that long. Not after last night, and a few minutes earlier.

"Soon," I countered. I needed more of her. In my house. In my bed. Like this when there wasn't anything between us. No past. No jobs or school or shitty and non-existent parents.

I'd never had this before and I liked it, which was fucking crazy.

She shook her head. "There's no time. I should've been studying last night and now I'm behind."

I wasn't going to tell her that she definitely shouldn't have been studying, that fucking me was a much better option, but she'd been stupid and gone to the warehouse alone.

Once dressed, she came over, wrapped a hand around my neck, leaned down and kissed me. "Thanks for the lessons," she whispered.

I let her go, let her walk out the front door. Because this wasn't a thing. This wasn't a relationship. It was what I wanted, right?

12

EAST

"You're sure he's fine?" I asked West.

When he'd called me two hours ago that South had been shot, I told Valerie I had a family emergency and ran out of the building so fast I broke the hinges on the exit door. I didn't take the time to check on it, but I'd track down the maintenance man later.

I'd pulled up to the ER near the ranch and abandoned my truck in the drop off lane. West met me just outside the sliding doors. "I told you on the way he hadn't been shot after all. It was Maisey's sister who took the bullet."

He had told me that, but I hadn't believed him.

Okay, I had believed him, but it hadn't eased my panic or had me drive any slower. I'd gotten close with North, South, and West... and Jed Barnett since Macon died. Closer than we'd ever been before, and that old bond had been forged in mutual misery. Not in very much else. But in the months since the fucker was put in the ground, we had each other's backs. Today was not the day for losing one of them.

I might fight with my hands, but I couldn't dodge fucking bullets and neither could they.

"Who the hell is Maisey?" I asked, taking a deep breath and relaxing my shoulders.

He took off his Stetson and ran a hand through his hair. His constant calm was a fucking pain in my ass. "His woman."

"His what?" I asked, staring at my twin as if he told me South had a trained circus seal.

"It's his story to tell."

I circled my finger in the air, set my other hand on my hip. "Highlights would be great."

"Maisey is on the cleaning staff of the big house. South met her and that was it. She's got a crazy identical twin who likes to trade places, fuck Macon's *other* child and get shot."

"Maisey fucks who?" I ran a hand over my face.

When a car slowly pulled into the circle, we moved out of the way and I followed West inside the ER.

"Maisey fucks South," West said, clarifying. The older volunteer at the desk raised a brow at West's words and he tugged me toward a fake potted plant.

"Then who's Macon's other kid?" I asked, trying to keep up.

"Micah Cunningham. Maybe. He's a psycho who wants South dead so he can have the inheritance all to himself."

I blinked, stared at my brother. "Are you fucking kidding me?"

He set his hat back on his head. "Nope. I can't make this shit up."

North and Jed came through the ER entrance. North saw us first and Jed led her our way with his hand at the small of her back. She was in jeans, sweater and her hair was piled on top of her head. Jed looked more cowboy than head of security for a billion-dollar company. Where West was chill, Jed was ruthlessly calm. One easygoing, the other choosing to be calm so all the shit he'd dealt with at his job didn't crush him.

North hugged me.

It had been three weeks since the night Ella came

to the fights and I'd taken her to my bed. Since then the demons that haunted me weren't as bad. I wasn't as angry or frustrated. I hadn't fought again at that shitty warehouse, only working out and sparring at the gym. Although West's call about South pushed me right to the brink again. Instead of beating the shit out of someone, I was here, waiting to see my brother for myself.

Somehow, Ella had… soothed me. Ridiculous sounding but sharing my need to fight with her made it easier. Especially since she seemed to understand. We came from completely different worlds and yet we both had shitty childhoods. Had pasts that haunted us. I knew she did, but she hid it well. Pushed people away and avoided relationships for similar reasons.

Which made us perfect for each other. Which made me want a relationship because we both didn't want one.

Yeah, it made no fucking sense.

Ella had been too busy to meet up again, no matter how much I wanted her back in my bed. She left class before I could initiate any kind of talk. She worked in the math office, but we talked only about department related topics. No more panty collection in the copy room.

Nothing. Which had me rubbing one out in the shower way too fucking often.

"I'm good," I told her finally. "Where's South?"

Jed set a hand on North's shoulder. "He's in with Maisey," he told me. West had said Jed had been at South's place right after it all happened, whatever that was exactly. If anyone knew something, it was Jed. "I talked with the sheriff and Cunningham will get checked out and then head right to the county lockup to wait for arraignment."

"I thought he was the one with the gun. What happened to him?" I asked.

"South," Jed said, with his usual cool demeanor. "Beating the shit out of people seems to be a Wainright trait."

West pointed past North. "There he is."

I followed the others to the main desk and met South there. He held a woman's hand. I pegged her to be close in age to Ella, maybe younger. Brown hair, glasses. Short. She was pretty but had nothing on Ella whose fiery hair and green eyes were like a sucker punch every time she looked my way.

"Everything okay?" North asked, glancing from South to Maisey and back.

"All good," South said, clutching Maisey as if he were afraid she'd vanish if he let go. "The lump's a fluid filled cyst. By the way, we're getting married."

What the fuck? North blinked. Jed eyed South.

West's mouth hung open and I could only stare and try to process. He wasn't shot but engaged.

"South!" Maisey snapped, smacking South. "They didn't need to know about the lump. God."

"I'm... I-" North sputtered. "Congratulations about both!"

She hugged Maisey.

"Welcome to the family," she added. "I'm excited to have a sister after being stuck with these three morons. You can tell me about these cysts and I won't blab about them like South. Girl talk. I hear it's a thing."

"I'd... I'd like that."

West hugged Maisey next. "Nice job," he said, obviously pleased that someone had claimed and hopefully tamed our moody brother. Where I was angry, South was definitely as moody as a fourteen-year-old girl.

"I'm East, by the way," I said finally, moving to stand in front of them but mock glaring at South. "No manners. Maybe you can teach this caveman some."

I gave Maisey a light hug. I had no idea if lump-exams needed any recovery time.

I needed to spend more time at the ranch if South could find a woman and ask her to marry him between my visits. But if he did like West had said and took one look at Maisey and fell for her, maybe it was a family thing. North fell for Jed over Macon's casket. I'd met up with them in the foyer during the wake. I'd had a sandwich in hand and they'd been glaring and staring, practically eye fucking each other with the entire town in attendance.

"She likes when I'm a caveman," South said, and shoved me playfully. "Stop hugging my woman."

I stepped back, held my hands up. Yeah, I could totally relate. That handsy asshole at the fight had been touching Ella and I'd finished my opponent to get to her. I hadn't stopped thinking about that, which meant my jealousy lingered. Made me wonder if Ella didn't have time for me because she was spending it with someone else, like Mr. Handsy.

"I'm glad your sister is okay," North said.

"She jumped in front of a bullet for us," Maisey replied, then looked up at South. Yeah, they were fucking tight. Another pang of jealousy hit me in the chest like an uppercut.

Since when did I want that? Love? A connection with a woman? I wasn't interested in Maisey. It was Ella I wanted to look at me that way.

"Jed told me about the evil twin," I said, trying to *not* think about Ella, which was pretty much impossible. "Although the taking-a-bullet thing might make her a little less evil. Either way, I had to come see for myself." I didn't want either of them to know how half-crazed I'd been. But South was more than fine, although I wanted to connect with Jed to find out everything about this Cunningham guy. He'd know every detail. Anything that affected North–even tangentially through one of us–and he was on it.

I pointed at West. "If there's any doubt, between us, he's the evil twin."

West rubbed his hands together and grinned. "Sounds fun."

"I also came to make sure you and South are okay," I added. "You scared the shit out of me."

"It's good to see your face," South told me. Yeah, the feeling was mutual. "Just so you know, staying with me this year for the holidays is out."

I laughed and thumbed toward West. "I'll stay at the bachelor pad."

That didn't sound all that fun. Seeing Maisey and South had me craving the holidays with Ella. Getting to know her away from campus without prying eyes. Without rules or classes. Like we had that one night.

That didn't make a relationship, that made time alone with her. A few days escape. Nothing more. Although when South leaned down and kissed the top of Maisey's head, I wondered if that was all I wanted.

Because South knew Maisey was his and she was safe in his arms.

Now that I knew he wasn't shot full of holes, I wanted to head back to town and track down Ella. These past few weeks had been painfully slow and... fucking lonely. I wanted to pull her into my arms and never let her go. How the hell did I do that without a relationship?

13

ELLA

I'D CRAVED East since spending the night with him weeks ago. No other guy would do, especially *not* RJ. I'd never slept–actually slept in a bed–with another person before, not as a child or since. Especially not with a hot guy whose body created enough heat and coziness that a down comforter wasn't needed. And definitely not naked.

East had been bossy and naughty and... I thought more about what we'd done than reading chapters of my textbooks trying to study. That made me nervous because it meant I liked it too much. It wasn't something that could last. I didn't do relationships and East had made it clear he didn't either. The sex was good. *Really* good, except I had nothing to compare it to.

It couldn't be average because if it got any better, I'd die from too much pleasure.

Was I craving dick, or East? Was it the fact that I was finally having sex that my libido was awake and revving or East himself? I had no idea, and my roommates weren't the ones to ask. Well, they were because they knew everything about fucking and forgetting. Except I couldn't tell them about East. He was a secret.

God, I'd been the one to break my own rules going to that underground fight night. I'd followed him and it had led to sharing his bed. Having sex while we were student and professor.

It had also led to bumping into RJ at the fight and him finding me now. Here, on campus. He stood by a bicycle rack and stepped toward me.

I'd had my head tucked down to keep the blowing snow off my face. The flakes were fat and falling fast, but the snowplows were staying ahead of it. The streets were wet, but clear. This was Montana, not some southern town that had empty grocery stores because of a whisper of an upcoming cold snap.

I froze and others who came out of the building had to move around me. Realizing I was slowing people down, I moved off to the side and glanced around. "What are you doing here?" I asked, suddenly panicked.

My puffy coat was too warm all of a sudden and the campus, which I'd always thought of as safe, felt... tainted. The sick feelings of Ron's attention came rushing back. I knew he was dead and couldn't touch me, but RJ was a reminder of it all. And he was here, which meant he'd hunted me down. It wasn't another coincidence.

He was in the same heavy canvas jacket but had a beanie on his head. Snow had settled on the top which meant he'd been waiting for a bit. "You didn't stick around after the fights to catch up," he said.

He and all the spectators in the warehouse had seen East toss me over his shoulder and carry me off. What no one saw was us leaving together, or at least that I knew of. Although perhaps RJ had after all.

"How did you find me?" I asked.

He shrugged, although it was barely noticeable through his coat. "There was talk about the fighter being a professor here."

Oh shit. He *had* tracked me down through East.

"Okay, well, good seeing you," I said, starting to walk away. Needing to get as far from him as possible.

Except RJ set his hand on my arm to stop me.

I glanced over my shoulder, but refused to look at

him head on. He'd been in that hell house, had known what was going on. Or at least had an idea. He was Ron's son, had his blood in him. My thoughts immediately went to East and how he'd said his father had been a bad man and how East had thought he had his tainted blood.

Was RJ like his father? Was he here to pick up after his dad? I wasn't underage any longer, but neither was RJ.

"I haven't stopped thinking about you," he admitted. "Since the fire."

I swallowed, bile rising in my throat. I'd desperately left that all behind. Blocked it from my mind like building a brick wall around my thoughts. While I hadn't been looked at by the police for the incident—it had quickly been decided carelessness and drunkenness were to blame for the fire and Ron's death—it followed me wherever I went. I'd thought it was staying in my past, except now RJ was here. Knew all about it. He'd been there too.

My foster care records were sealed so no one, not even RJ, could have tracked me down from any scrap of info before I turned eighteen. Maybe that was why he hadn't appeared until now, the miserable coincidence of both of us being at the fights.

"Okay, well, I don't think back on that time. Please

let me go." I glanced down at his hand and he dropped it from my coat as if it were on fire. I was safe here. People were all around us getting to classes. He wasn't actually doing anything wrong. I could scream and call for help, but from what exactly? I'd have to tell campus police about my past.

"Go out with me."

I took a step back. *Go out with him?* God, no. RJ embodied every nightmare I carried. Just looking at him was a visual reminder of his father. I hadn't liked RJ as a kid. He'd always been quiet, but he watched me. I wanted nothing to do with him now.

"No. Sorry. Bye, RJ."

I dashed off, not looking back, leaving him behind. Again.

By the time I got to my car, I was sweating and breathing as if I'd run a marathon. All I could see or think about was RJ and his family in the house on Cedar Avenue.

"Whoa, there."

I startled and stifled a scream when someone stepped in front of me.

It wasn't RJ this time, but East.

I froze once again, only the lingering fear of RJ making my blood rush in my ears. My fingers tingled with the sudden rush of adrenaline.

"Jesus, are you okay?" he asked, studying me. He leaned down a bit so we were eye level.

I nodded, swallowed hard.

It was clear in his eyes, the way he glanced around the lot, that he wanted to protect me from whatever had me panicking or grab me and hug me. Instead, he shoved his hands in pant's pockets.

"What's wrong?"

I couldn't tell East about RJ. To him, he was just a handsy rando from the fight. If he knew a guy from that event had tracked me down to campus through him, he might go all Incredible Hulk, rip his clothes to bits and track RJ down. While the ridiculous idea made me calm a bit, I couldn't share the truth.

Ron, RJ and my past was exactly that. In. My. Past. I couldn't tell East about how I'd let Ron die. That it was my fault he'd burned to death. I could have dragged him to safety or told the firefighters he was still in the house. I'd done nothing which was accomplice enough.

Not only was it probably illegal, but it went against every principle of being a social worker. Of helping others. It wouldn't go down well with my grad school application if my history was known. Besides, East was my professor and nothing more.

He wasn't my boyfriend. I didn't bare my soul to

him. I just let him lick my pussy and fuck it until I screamed.

I gave him a shaky smile. He seemed to be very perceptive when it came to me. No matter what he said otherwise, he was protective. A new car battery was proof of that. “Nothing. I’m just getting behind and I was in a rush.”

His gaze darted about again. “I haven’t been able to talk to you.”

My plan had worked then. But now that I saw him, that I could pick up his clean scent even in the snow, I felt like I’d missed out.

“I wanted to see what you were doing for Thanksgiving.”

I frowned. “Thanksgiving?”

He nodded. Snowflakes fell on his hair, his shoulders. Wasn’t he cold? Of course not.

“I’m spending it at the ranch.” He reached up, ran a hand over the back of his neck. “I thought you might want to come, since–”

“Since I don’t have family.”

He gave me a small smile. “Yeah. I mean, unless you have other plans. Going home with a girlfriend or something.”

I hadn’t in the past. I’d always spent it alone, taking the free time to pick up extra shifts at work or getting ahead on my studying. That was my intention this year as well.

"I thought... this isn't a relationship," I said, looking around and lowering my voice. "Meeting your family changes things."

He shrugged. "Yeah, not a relationship. You're right. My sister will definitely get the wrong idea." He took a step toward me, but a few feet still remained. He couldn't reach out and touch me. "I'm impatient."

I was impressed he admitted it. I felt the same way. But the longer I waited, the longer I could convince myself that having sex with East was going to remain just that. Sex. A weekend with him far from campus was way more than just sex, no matter how much we had.

No matter how much I craved the thought of spending the holiday with others, especially East and his family, I couldn't. I wouldn't.

I didn't want to like being with East. I didn't want to know what being with a family was like. I was fine not knowing. Sure, I knew I was missing out, but experiencing it proved what I didn't have. It didn't give me feelings of happiness and belonging that I would crave in the future.

I was used to being alone. Content.

"Thanks for the offer, but I can't. Work." It was my usual excuse and easy to toss out.

He nodded, then stepped back. There was nothing else he could say or do. "Right. Well, let me know if you change your mind."

I offered him a small smile and a nod and got out of there before I did just that.

14

ELLA

I SPENT the rest of the week picturing East standing in the snow. I never used to be a daydreamer, but now I was, which meant I was behind. For every hour I read my textbooks and wrote papers, probably half of it was spent staring at nothing. Imagining East's bare body. The feel of his short hair beneath my fingers. The deep sound of his voice. The sure thrusts of his hips.

I was fucked, and these days, not by him.

Giggling came before my roommates into the apartment. I was sitting on my bed, my legs folded with my laptop and studying stuff in front of me. It was the Tuesday before Thanksgiving. Finals weren't for a few more weeks so many teachers went easy on assignments prior to the holiday since so many travelled. Or at least that was what it seemed. I used the time to buckle down and get ahead.

Not Sarah, Leah, and Lynn. To them, it was another night to party before they went home to their families. Sarah hopped a plane to Colorado, Leah drove to Salt Lake and Lynn to Missoula.

"Yes, we'll go to that party. First I need to change my shoes."

Sarah.

"Babe, you look amazing just as you are. I'm going to get them off of you later anyway."

A guy.

Sarah giggled again because she intended to let him get her out of her boots, and everything else, later.

"Hey, Ella," Sarah called, gliding past my door and to her room.

"Hi," I replied, turning back to my work.

"What's your major?"

I looked up, ready to answer, then the words got caught in my throat.

It was RJ.

"Um..." I glanced around, panicked and confused. Why was he here, and with Sarah?

"Well?" he asked, a smile I knew could sway a

woman to do things. Probably getting Sarah out of her boots. Had they slept together?

"Sociology," I replied, although the word was scraped out.

He lifted his chin. "You were always the smart one."

The reminder of our joint past had me seeing red. "What are you doing here?" I hissed.

"You wouldn't go out with me, so I had to think of a different way to get close to you." He leaned his shoulder against my open doorway.

My mouth fell open. O.M.G. He was crazy.

"By dating my roommate?" I whispered. I was sure Sarah knew nothing about the connection I had with RJ, who to her was just a cute guy.

"I wanted you then, EllBell and I want you now. You just got away from me for a little while."

I hadn't heard that nickname in years and it made me nauseated.

"You won't get away this time," he added.

The words were spoken so casually, but they were scary as fuck.

"All set!" Sarah said, coming to stand right beside RJ. She looked into my room, took in my ragged sweats and sloppy hair, my studying pile. Nothing unusual to her.

RJ stroked a hand down her back.

"What's going on?" Sarah asked. She had long blonde hair, artfully curled beneath a hat with a huge pink pompom on top. Her jacket was a shiny gray and her jeans had a tear at the knee she probably paid extra for. She had on different boots, these with fur edging at the top. She looked like a ski bunny who didn't know how to ski but spent her day in the lodge drinking spiked cocoa.

While she might be flighty and wanted her major to be partying, she wasn't stupid.

"Your friend was saying hi," I told her, pasting on a smile and keeping my gaze on Sarah. I refused to look at RJ. My fingers remained clenched together. I didn't want either of them to see they were shaking, to let RJ know how he got to me.

Sarah glanced between us.

"It's cool that she likes to study," RJ told Sarah. "But she should come with us to the party."

From the look on Sarah's face, the idea of me as a third wheel was as bad as her shoveling snow around the trash dumpster.

"Ella doesn't party," Sarah said, making it clear to me that I definitely wasn't partying with her tonight.

"I've got a paper to finish," I said, tapping my laptop screen.

Sarah's smile brightened at my agreement.

"Not all weekend," RJ countered. That grin was still in place.

Sarah's spine stiffened. I wanted to puke.

Sarah tugged on his arm. "The others are waiting for us."

He looked down at Sarah. "Sure, babe. Let's go."

Sarah led the way down the hall and before RJ followed, he winked at me. "See you around, Ella."

I heard the promise and I started to shake. Not only had RJ found me, but he'd gotten in my apartment, in my roommate's bed. He knew she and the others were going to be away for the holiday weekend. Knew I wasn't.

Had he gotten a key? Sarah wasn't stupid enough to give one to a guy, but if he was spending time with her only to get closer to me, then I wouldn't put it past him to make a copy.

Which meant I wasn't safe here because he'd be back after my roommates went home for the weekend. I had no place to go. No money for a hotel. No parents or grandparents to stay with. I–

My heart leapt at the idea, the hope. East. He'd invited me to spend the break with him and his family. It was a bad idea since so much was on the line. Having him replace a car battery could be explained away easily enough if someone mentioned it. Even a ride to and from work. But spending a holiday at his house?

I should care. But I didn't. Not now. At this point, there was dangerous and there was *dangerous.*

I wasn't afraid of East, only what could happen if we got together.

I was petrified of RJ. Especially since he'd done nothing wrong. I couldn't go to the police. I'd pretty much killed his dad. I couldn't complain about a stalker because I was a college kid. He was my age. I hadn't seen him in years until recently. The trend was too short to be considered stalking.

He was having sex with Sarah. Not me.

I wasn't going to stick around to find out what he planned next. I couldn't.

My cell was beside my laptop. I grabbed it. East had texted me that night my battery had died so I had his number if I ever needed it. Now was the time.

With shaky fingers, I texted him. *Invitation for the weekend still open?*

I sat there, tried to calm my breathing as I waited. Fortunately, I didn't have to wait long. It pinged in my hand.

Any chance you can leave in the morning?

Tears filled my eyes from the relief.

Yes.

I had one class tomorrow, but I'd skip it. I'd get notes from someone. Work was closed on Thanksgiving and I was scheduled to work Friday and Saturday. I'd call in sick, which I never did. Tell them food poisoning, bad turkey or something. It would be a hit to my bank account, but at this point, I'd eat ramen for a month to avoid RJ.

I slammed my laptop shut, shoved it into my bag along with my papers.

Nine. My place.

I responded with a thumbs up emoji, then got to packing, because I wasn't staying here a second longer than I had to.

15

EAST

When I heard Ella's car come down the driveway, I went out to meet her. She rolled down her window for me, just like she had that day her battery died.

Her text had thrilled me. I hadn't expected it because she was opposed to us being together. And yet she'd been *very* happy here after the fight. She'd let her walls down and let me in, then built them right back up again. I had to wonder if there was a reason why she'd changed her mind, or if she was as impatient as me to be together.

It was my own reaction that surprised me. I was

fucking thrilled she wanted to go to the ranch with me.

An entire weekend, not just a night in my bed. Or even a quick fuck over Mike's desk.

I didn't understand my interest in her. My obsession. Maybe it was because I couldn't have her. No, *shouldn't.* She should be out of reach, untouchable, at least until the end of the semester. Maybe it was that that had me craving her.

I'd spend the weekend with her, get her out of my system. It didn't make a relationship. It didn't make her my girlfriend. Only a weekend.

Right?

"Hey. You can pull your car into the garage. That way if it snows, we won't have to dig it out."

She nodded, her green eyes roving over my face. I went to the keypad on the side of the garage and entered the code. The double doors rose and she drove in.

I grabbed her bag after she pulled it from the back seat.

When she slammed her door shut and turned to face me, I couldn't help but kiss her. Sure, my neighbors could be watching, but they'd need binoculars. The one thing about Montanans was they liked to be left alone, which meant in most cases, they left others alone in return.

We weren't near the campus and while it was daylight, I wasn't waiting a second longer to get my lips on hers.

She gasped as I pulled her against me, laughed when I hauled her up so her feet were dangling in the air so our mouths were at the same height. Then moaned when my tongue found hers.

My dick was instantly hard and all I wanted to do was drag her into the house for a quickie, but there wasn't time. From a distance, I heard the rotors of the helicopter as it approached and I set Ella down.

"You ready to go?" I asked.

She nodded, her lips glossy and her cheeks flushed. "Sure."

The approach got louder and the wind kicked up. "Good, because our ride's here."

Her eyes widened as the helicopter came into view then landed in my yard. The pilot had been here before and was familiar with the power line placement—on the far edge of the property—and set down easily.

Her mouth dropped open. "We're taking a helicopter?"

Yeah, no one flew around in them. Except North

when she went to work most days. Besides bad weather, that was how she got from the ranch to the company's headquarters in Billings.

I could have driven, but I figured this would be a treat for Ella. Hell, it was for me too. Technically, I could use it anytime, but I never did. I wanted to be East Wainright, PhD, not the billionaire. But pulling out a helicopter for holiday travel proved I couldn't escape that entirely.

Seeing the excitement on Ella's face made me feel good about my decision. I tugged down her winter hat and kissed her swiftly. I wasn't used to seeing to another's happiness. Not that I was an asshole or anything, but I didn't get close to people. Ella was changing that.

The pilot didn't turn off the engine, only gave me the signal it was safe to approach.

"Ready?" I asked, my voice loud so she could hear me.

Her hair swirled around her face as she nodded.

I grabbed her hand. "Duck down and follow me."

ELLA

. . .

"We're still finding pieces of metal out in the field," South said, shaking his head as if he were surprised. I had no idea what he meant.

North laughed. "Yeah, maybe shooting up Macon's plaques and trophies wasn't the smartest idea."

"Scared the shit out of me. I thought you were being murdered," Jed said, leaning back in his chair and setting his arm along the back of North's.

The way they looked at each other was... wow. They were together, as in solid. Permanent. Jed with his dark hair and beard, North all blonde and gorgeous. I'd only met them a little while ago when they'd returned from work. Since East had used the helicopter, his sister and boyfriend had driven to their company's office, returning in time for dinner.

That their chef had made.

A chef!

We were sitting at the kitchen table–that could seat ten–eating some kind of chicken casserole with mushrooms and noodles. With wine. And beer. And what I thought were homemade rolls. It was all delicious and I was stuffed.

Besides North and Jed, South and his fiancée, Maisey, were there. So was East's twin West. The siblings looked nothing alike, although I remembered that South was technically only a half-sibling.

Everyone was casually dressed–North had changed out of some blatantly expensive power suit for yoga pants and a university math hoodie, probably a gift from East. Jed and West looked like Marlboro men without the cigarettes and South had a burn hole in his flannel. Maisey was quiet and cute with glasses that kept slipping down her nose.

The helicopter had made me think they would be stuffy and pretentious. Because… helicopter! I'd thought East's tricked out truck was fancy. I figured them all to be obnoxious like in movies depicting rich, self-involved assholes, yet none of them were. Over dinner I learned Jed had been in the FBI until recently. South was a sculptor. West a rancher. Maisey had been a house cleaner–*this* house–until the month before when South took one look at her and decided she was his. North was the only one with a high-powered job.

Except they were all down to earth. Normal.

What wasn't normal was the house. Mansion. Epically large western homestead that had more rooms than I could count. The helicopter had landed in a field, so there wasn't an official landing pad, although if we weren't in rural Montana, they'd probably have one. There was a pool, winterized now until summer. A guest house, where East and I would be staying. A guest house. As if the big house didn't have enough bedrooms.

East had told me the place had been built at the turn of the last century by a great, great grandparent, with sections added on through the generations. It was beautiful, all log and river rock, glossy wood floors and antiques. The fireplace in the great room was roaring and the kitchen was… cozy.

I'd never been in a place like it. I could live here. Hell, who wouldn't? Except there wasn't anything around for miles. No neighbors. Candace from school had said they were the largest landowners in the state. That meant what we flew over probably belonged to the Wainrights. Every beautiful, desolate acre.

Maisey, who was on my right, leaned in. "Pretty crazy, right? This place?" she whispered.

I nodded, blushing for being caught out.

"There's even a telephone room. I'm still getting used to it. The fanciness of it. To me luxury is having applesauce with my boxed mac and cheese." South tugged her toward him, and he put his lips to her forehead.

Meanwhile, West replied to North. "Only Macon's shit was killed that night. If there's anything else we missed, we'll have South add it to one of his sculptures."

I still had no idea what they were talking about and it must have shown on my face. "After Macon died, we cleaned out the bookshelves of his golf and community awards and did some skeet shooting," East explained.

"With the help of a little whiskey," West added.

"Have we been good and waited long enough?" North asked, glancing between me and East.

East sat back and sighed, turning to me. "Can my sister ask all the questions now?"

Suddenly I felt a little panicked with everyone looking my way.

"Shit, you're going to make her run for the hills," West said.

"Okay, but why?" I asked.

"He's never brought a woman before."

My eyebrows went up. Never? Then why me? That's what I wondered as I stared at him. Except he didn't do relationships, so it made sense, but again, why me?

"A cat once," West said.

East tipped his head back and laughed. "That's right. Felix. I offered to watch my college roommate's cat. He escaped the guest house, met up with a feral tabby in the barn, fell in love, had eleven kittens and lived happily ever after."

I eyed him, wondering if he was messing with me. I glanced at West. "It happened."

I laughed, enjoying their easy banter and the ridiculous stories. "It's fine, North. Go for it. But I might need the help of a little whiskey."

East grinned at how I'd picked up on West's earlier words and stroked his hand over my hair, then leaned in. "I want you sober. For later."

I could feel my cheeks heat again and my nipples hardened at what he might have planned. I had a pretty good idea.

"Whatever he just told her, I want you to do it to me later," Maisey told South.

I covered my face with my hands. I wasn't used to sibling banter. It was all in jest, but well meant.

"I'll start easy," North said, who seemed to have single minded focus.

I couldn't hide behind my hands like a four-year-old, so I dropped them and nodded at North.

"Why East?" North asked. She reached for a roll and set it on her plate. "I mean, he's big and brawny and can calculate the square root of six-hundred twenty-seven in his head."

"Twenty-five and a little leftover," East replied, then winked at North, who rolled her eyes.

South threw a napkin at East and it bounced off his head.

I couldn't help but smile. I liked this. I liked them. They were... fun and an example of what a family should be like. Since I'd never had parents, the fact that they didn't have any didn't seem like something was missing.

North looked to me expectantly. I wasn't going to see them again after this weekend, so I figured I might as well be myself.

I glanced at East, held his gaze. He was waiting as well.

"Why East?" I repeated. "He has a big dick and knows how to use it."

"That's right," East murmured, then gave me a sly grin that had me wanting to hand him my panties.

Everyone else was silent for a moment and then started to laugh. I didn't look away from East, but I heard Jed say, "You asked, princess."

"Well played, doll," East murmured, then looked at North, a smirk on his lips. "Don't ask the question if you don't want to know the answer."

It was her turn to cover her face. "I don't want to know about any of my brothers' sex lives, which is getting harder and harder. Two of you have found your women."

"And West's found his favorite sheep," South added jokingly.

"I'll tell you what's hard," East added and North groaned.

She shook herself and gave Ella a big smile. "Okay, a safer question. East said you're a student. What's your major?"

"Sociology."

She poked at the casserole on her plate and took a bite. "Because..."

"Because I want to be a social worker," I replied.

"I'm going back to school in January for nursing," Maisey told me.

"I spend my days with cows, not sheep," West added, reaching for the baking dish for another helping.

"He might need some counseling," East said playfully.

"Our philanthropic arm needs someone to run it," North said, wiping her mouth with her napkin.

My eyes widened. "You're... offering me a job?"

She shrugged. "I'm sure you want to get your degree first, but this would entail–"

"Princess, no work until Monday," Jed said, picking up his beer and taking a casual sip. The look between them made it seem as if she needed the reminder. While North pursed her lips, she nodded.

"Don't worry, I won't be graduating before Monday and I want to work with kids," I clarified. I was a little overwhelmed that over chicken casserole, the CEO of a billion-dollar company wanted me to work for her.

"I forgot to ask if you have to work this weekend," East murmured. He'd set his arm along the back of my chair as Jed had North's, and his hand cupped my neck. It was gentle, yet it felt possessive.

I liked it.

"Sunday." I wasn't going to tell him my plan to call in sick before then.

He glanced at my plate, then back at me. "You done?"

I couldn't eat another bite. I hadn't had a real home cooked meal in... ever.

"Yeah."

He pushed to his feet, his chair sliding across the wood floors. "We're out of here. What time are we eating turkey tomorrow?"

I stared up at him.

"We're having ham," North corrected. "Turns out, we all hate turkey."

He tugged me to my feet, keeping me close.

"What time?" he asked again.

"Five, but the game starts at two."

I didn't care much about football, but I'd laze about and watch.

"Screw football," East said.

"Meaning you're going to screw Cinderella," West clarified.

East pulled me toward the back door as he called over his shoulder, "And I thought I was the genius in the family. Brother, you need to find a woman of your own."

I looked back at East's family and gave them a wave, but East didn't slow for me to do anything more. I wasn't going to tell him I was as eager as he was to get naked. He'd find out soon enough.

16

EAST

I LIKED that she held her own with my family. Not that they would have messed with her. They weren't cruel. Hell, we all *knew* cruel and would never subject someone else to it. I would have stepped in if Ella had been bothered even a little.

When she'd told North all she wanted me for was my dick, I almost came in my pants. After I got myself under control, I realized *I* was the one slightly hurt. All she wanted me for was sex? That's what we'd said all along, what we'd based our... thing on. It didn't have a name. It wasn't a relationship. It wasn't a fling.

Still, I hadn't realized how much I wanted Ella

here at Billionaire Ranch with the others. They were the only ones whose opinions mattered to me. I knew they'd like her. I hadn't figured out what there wasn't to like. She could understand the shit we'd all been through with Macon.

Not in the exact way he'd held power over us, but she'd felt powerless herself.

At least I had this crowd. They were mine.

Whether I wanted them around or not.

Right now, it was not.

"East!" Ella laughed as I tugged her across the back patio, past the pool and to the guest house through the cold night.

Sometimes I stayed with South or West at their houses. Other times I stayed in the smaller house on the property. My grandfather had built it for my grandmother's extended family who would visit. While there were so many bedrooms in the main house, I guess he wanted the place all to himself and his bride.

I could understand. While I didn't mind ribbing North about my sex life, I didn't want to know about hers either. I wasn't kidding myself that she and Jed didn't go at it. Staying under separate roofs kept me from overhearing them.

And me in return. Because when I said I would see

them for Thanksgiving dinner, I meant it. I didn't plan on letting Ella out of bed until then.

I slowed my pace as she tried to keep up.

Only when I had the front door of the guest house closed behind us did I stop completely. And that was to press her against the wall and kiss the hell out of her. "Fuck, I've been waiting for this forever," I breathed.

I settled my forehead against hers as my hands skimmed her waist, slipping beneath the hem of her sweater to feel her warm, bare skin.

"I feel the same way," she replied, her lips sliding along my jaw. "East, I want you. And your really big dick."

I couldn't help but laugh. I used to hate to come to the ranch. The guest house wasn't far enough away from Macon for me. It would be torture, but North had needed me around–I hadn't realized how much until recently–so I'd endured. I never imagined bringing a woman here. I'd never measured up to Macon's ridiculous ruler of success. I'd never subject a girlfriend to him.

Girlfriend?

Hell, the title didn't matter. Ella was here, liked my family and I had her tits cupped in my palms.

“Ready for your next lesson, Miss Taynor?” I asked, running my thumbs over her already hard nipples.

She moaned and arched her back. “Yes, sir.”

That went right to my dick.

“I’ll let you choose which area of study you want to work on tonight. Taking my dick down your throat, a little bondage, or some ass play. I know you’ll excel at any of them.”

I watched her, making sure what I offered got her hot. I wouldn’t do anything that she wasn’t into. What Ella needed, I’d give to her. She was a recent virgin, so butt stuff might have pushed her a little, but the way her cheeks flushed and her eyes got all hazy, it was clear none of my suggestions were a turnoff.

Her hands dropped to my belt and she yanked it open. “Is there an option D, all of the above?”

Holy. Fuck.

17

ELLA

RETURNING TO WORK WAS TOUGH. East showed me a life that I could easily get used to. At a young age I recognized the difference between poor and *poor.* In all of the foster families I'd been with, the parents worked. Some harder than others. Some had foster kids solely for the money. I was one of the ways they'd earned a living.

I knew early on I needed to rise above that. To rely on myself in all things, including money. A middle school English teacher told me I could be anything I wanted if I put my mind on my studies. Mrs. Torrez had said that being smart was what got someone ahead. I never forgot her or her words and encouragement. So instead of thinking about how miserable I was, I studied, because no one could take what I learned from me.

I had goals. I wanted a home of my own. A crockpot. Flannel sheets. I wanted a job that could pay for all of it. A job that helped others. I hadn't considered much more. Never imagined being rich.

But Wainright wealth was something else entirely.

A helicopter. A guest house. A chef. House cleaners. Room after room of fancy and expensive things that no one noticed.

Besides the ham dinner for Thanksgiving, East kept me to himself. No matter how much North and Maisey had wanted to pull me into a girls' night while I was there, East had been selfish with me.

I hadn't minded at all.

I napped. God, did I nap. I slept late. I was woken up with East's head between my thighs or sprawled across his chest. We laughed and talked. Binge watched TV and ate leftovers he raided from the big house's fridge.

I'd been too relaxed. Too coddled. Too sexed. Because Sunday afternoon when I went back to the warehouse for work, it was the first time I saw it differently. Filling boxes wasn't a means to an end, part of my big master plan, but drudgery.

And I didn't like how I felt about it.

I wasn't supposed to change for a man. I never expected to change in this way. I didn't have the luxury to rethink anything. I had six months until graduation. Then grad school. I was getting by. I had income coming in. I could pay my bills. I had a roof over my head, food in my belly. And no one telling me what to do.

That had been enough.

But now? Now I wanted East, too. Not just his fancy helicopter either.

I wanted him.

I actually liked the guy and not for his sexual prowess.

Except I couldn't have him. Couldn't want him because that meant I'd rely on someone, even emotionally.

So when I trudged across the big parking lot to my car after my shift, I was equally thrilled and panicked when East's big truck was there. He hopped out when he saw me.

"Hey," he said, reaching for me and pulling me into him.

"What are you doing here?" I asked, reveling in the feel of being in his arms.

Other employees were in the lot as well, but no one cared what I was up to.

"Wanted to make sure you got to your car safe."

That was sweet.

I hated it.

"You can't do this," I told him. The words tasted like ash on my tongue, but I had to say it. Eight hours of packing boxes had made the differences between us clear. It wasn't just that we should wait until the end of the semester to have sex. That ship had sailed. No matter how many times I said I didn't want a relationship, I still fell for him. That wasn't supposed to happen. I couldn't like it. I couldn't like him.

"Why not?"

"Because this isn't a thing. Us."

"We did a lot of *things* this weekend." He winked and gave me a sly smile, which made me melt like an icy sidewalk and he was salt being spread over it.

"It's just sex," I lied. "I can't have you thinking this is more than what we've always said."

"No relationships." When he'd originally agreed, he was fortified in that statement. Now he said it like he regretted even mentioning it.

I nodded. "I can't be in one."

"Can't or won't?" he asked.

"You agreed," I said instead of answering.

"I'm a math professor, not pre-law. It wasn't like we put it in writing."

I closed my eyes and breathed in, picking up his clean scent on the bitter cold air. "Then you see things in black and white. A relationship puts a variable in the mix. If this, then this." I waved my mittened hands in the air.

"So?" He looked confused and frustrated.

"So if I have a relationship with you, then I could be kicked out of school."

"Fine. I'll stay away for the rest of the semester. It's two weeks, but I'll do it."

"What then?" I countered. "People will still talk. I'll still be in school. Working here. Your life and mine will never mesh."

He stepped back, eyed me. "The helicopter was a little much?"

I nodded, although I'd loved every second of it.

He retreated again. "I'll go. For now. But I'm not letting you get away."

I won't let you get away this time.

The words were almost identical to what RJ had said to me in my apartment. I had tried to push thinking of him out of my mind when I was at the ranch with East, but his words were like a bucket of ice water. A wakeup call that I didn't have a problem with East. I had a problem with my past coming back to haunt me.

That clarity was what had me telling him, "It won't work. It's great, but I only want sex. Nothing more."

Because no matter how hard it was to say those lies, I couldn't let East find out about my past. With RJ around, East had to stay away. If he learned the truth, he'd be running away.

"You don't mean that," East said. "Because what we have is different."

I blinked back tears and nodded. "I have to go. I'm behind on my studying."

I turned and fled, climbing into my car and leaving East standing in the lot.

EAST

"Professor Wainright, this is Dean Simmons."

"Hello, Dean," I replied. She'd called me while I was at my desk, pretending to work on my latest paper.

I wasn't getting anything accomplished after Ella told me it wouldn't work. I did everything from stare blindly at my computer screen to pacing, deciding if I was more pissed off that she wasn't willing to give us a shot, or at myself because I'd actually started to want an "it." I wanted to be with Ella. A relationship. A thing. An *it*.

I shouldn't. I wasn't worthy of her. I couldn't give her what the guy in a relationship was supposed to. I didn't know how. I didn't *do* love.

Yet here I was in my office acting like an idiot pining for her.

"A complaint has been filed against a student for trading improved grades for sexual favors."

The woman was in her fifties and no-nonsense, a quality needed to be a dean of a university of this size. But I'd met her at many campus functions and while she had to report to a college president and a board, she was also fair and down to earth.

Her words gave me pause. And concern. And a fuckton of anger.

She was talking about Ella and me. She just hadn't gotten to it yet. I immediately went through all my interactions with Ella on campus. Besides the one time in the copy room, we'd been completely professional. If it had been the time she'd slipped me her panties, the dean would've called me much sooner. That had been weeks ago.

"Oh?"

"Ella Taynor is in your statistics class. While I know you are filling in for Dr. Newburgh, your behavior toward those students must be impeccable."

"Go on." I wasn't going to admit to anything. As I'd told Ella the night before, I wasn't a law professor, although I knew when to stay silent. Implicating myself meant confirming that Ella had done something wrong.

"The complaint included you, Doctor," she continued. "Your relationship with Miss Taynor specifically and the implications of that on her standing in the class."

"Where did this complaint come from?" I asked.

"I can't divulge that."

I gritted my teeth, took a moment. "I can't confirm or deny then what you are sharing is accurate. I am familiar with the non-fraternization policy the university has, but it isn't against the law."

"You are correct. However what is called into question is the validity of Miss Taynor's grade in that class. If it is found she sought favors to improve it, then she has broken the ethics rules and will be expelled."

Fuck. I set my elbow on my desk and leaned into

my palm. It was exactly what Ella had been concerned about.

"Based on your complaint, there is no finding of fault or consequence on my part? This concern is solely focused upon Miss Taynor?" The student sought out the teacher was the MO, it seemed.

"If you gave improved grades, then your actions will be scrutinized, of course," she added.

"So Miss Taynor has to prove her innocence."

This went against the American way. Usually, the prosecution had to prove her guilt. The way the dean was spinning this, it was the other way around.

"I will let you know what is discovered," she added. "Because we are so close to the end of the semester, a hearing will be on Wednesday."

Only two days for this shit to get figured out.

"Thank you, Dean," I said.

She hung up first. I stared at the white wall thinking about everything she said, then finally set the receiver down. Fuck. Fuck!

I wanted to text Ella, to check in with her, but it would be a paper trail of sorts. I had no idea how extensive the investigation went. Whether our communications or meetings would come into question. If the weekend we shared would become tainted with a lie.

Sure, we'd fucked. I'd definitely become attached. There was no relationship here, regardless of how much I wanted one, no matter how shitty I felt after our argument outside the shipping warehouse. Ella refused me, and now for a very obvious and valid reason.

Ella may have approached me in the bar, started all of this, but she wasn't in this alone. I was hooked on her, and I didn't want to be set free. I'd worried she'd break me, that being with her would make me reliant on someone. A virgin, at that! But I *was* reliant on her. I wanted her. Needed her. The idea of her stripped from my life was not something I even wanted to question.

Because while we'd both been fighting a relationship, we'd forged one. I would see it remain because Ella was worth it. Her dreams were mine to save.

I pulled my cell from my pocket. Called my future brother-in-law. I had a fight on my hands and this time it wasn't in the ring. "Jed, I need your help."

18

ELLA

THE SCHOOL HAD FOUND out about us. I pushed East away, and it still happened. Exactly as I worried it might. I felt sick and anxious, as if I needed to climb out of my own skin. I couldn't sit still, but I had nowhere to go.

When the dean called, I was between classes in the lobby of the sociology building, eating a sandwich I'd packed. There were tables and chairs for studying and more comfortable spots to sit and read. I was surrounded by other students, and yet the dean was loud in my ear, telling me I was up for an ethics violation, of a relationship with my professor in order to receive an improved grade.

I tossed my sandwich in the trash. What I'd eaten was lodged in my throat. Three years at the university and it came down to a math elective. It didn't matter that I'd been above reproach for every other class. This was the one they cared about.

East wouldn't have called me out. He was more into there being an *us* than I was. Did he do it as retaliation for turning him down the night before? That made no sense. He said he'd protect me. No, he wouldn't have done this. He only had to wait... less than two weeks. All he was doing was drawing potential disaster on himself as well.

I thought of the others in my class, if someone had it in for me. I wasn't close with anyone since it was a semester elective not in my major. The only time I'd connected with East outside of class had been that first day and we hadn't done anything. Only talked with the door open.

The car battery couldn't be an issue. Nothing could have been construed from that. I'd had a dead battery. He didn't push me over the engine and fuck me in the student lot!

I grabbed my bag so someone else could have my seat and paced. One wall was glass and it let in the sunshine, the snow reflecting brightly and I had to squint. Maybe it was someone in the math department? Someone who'd seen us in the copy room that day. Valerie? Again, why now?

I'd slept with my professor. That was true. But I'd never once considered asking him for a better grade in trade. East had never offered. We'd never even talked about the possibility. He knew how much my education meant and he wasn't a dick, or unethical. In fact, he was too nice. Sure, I'd surprised him with being a virgin, but he'd pointed out the door and my ability to walk away not only then but in the copy room too. I'd consented to everything we'd done. He'd been the one to push for it. Provided the condoms. He'd helped me with the car battery. Picked me up from work when I needed a ride. Protected me from–

Oh. My. God.

There, sitting on a bench on the concrete path toward the administration building was RJ. Watching me.

I stumbled back.

Fuck. It was him. He'd done this. It was obvious now. But why? I had to find out, so I dashed outside, my adrenaline pumping. The air was biting cold, but the sun helped. I didn't feel it. I didn't feel anything but anger.

"Why?" I said, pushing my bag up on my shoulder.

Slowly, he stood. "Hell Ellbell."

"Why?" I asked again.

He cocked his head. "I told you I'd never let you go."

"So you put in a complaint?" I hissed.

He shrugged. He looked like the typical student in his jeans and leather boots. Canvas jacket and ball cap. Except he wasn't. There was something wrong with him. Very wrong.

He looked normal, cool enough to get in Sarah's bed, but he was far from it. I'd spent the night at the apartment since my roommates were all back from the holiday weekend. RJ hadn't been there, thankfully. Now I knew why.

"You belong with me. You always did. I love you."

My mouth fell open as I stared at him, wide eyed. "What are you talking about? I haven't seen you in years!"

I wasn't shouting because everyone on campus didn't need to hear.

"I saw you," he said. "When you lived with us. You were so beautiful. Still are. You were meant to be mine. That's why I found you again at the fight."

He found me again because of a complete and horrible coincidence.

I frowned. “Then why are you lodging a complaint? It’s a lie.”

He smiled, but it was cold. “You sure about that? That professor of yours is a loose cannon. He shoved me, then tossed you over his shoulder.”

“You’re doing this because your ego got pushed around?”

“Everyone at the fight saw how crazy he was for you. Then you left with him.”

“There were creepy people there,” I said, hoping he’d catch my drift that I was referring to him. “He was protecting me.”

“Right. What about last weekend? Where did you spend it? I thought you were staying and studying?”

I shivered and not from the cold. “I went home with a friend.”

“Dr. Wainright.”

Arguing with him wasn’t going to work. Obviously, he knew I’d been with East. I’d gone to his house and taken a helicopter. While it wasn’t subtle, it hadn’t been anywhere near campus. Had he followed me to East’s house? He definitely couldn’t have followed to Billionaire Ranch.

“Why have me kicked out of school? It solves nothing.” That was what was going to happen. The dean had outlined the best and worst outcomes of a disciplinary hearing of this kind.

"Because you're mine." He stared at me with single minded focus. "School's keeping you from me. We'll leave here. Be together."

I backed away, retreated while I kept my eyes on him. He was scary as fuck.

"I'll tell him," he said. "About that night."

I froze. I knew exactly what he was talking about.

He closed the distance between us again and I refused to move. He brushed a finger down my cheek and I couldn't help but wince.

"How you didn't save my father from the fire."

Shit. *Shit.*

"I'll tell your lover how you're a murderer."

"I didn't set the fire," I said, my voice hollow. I hadn't spoken about that night with anyone. Not once. The social worker had come before dawn, before the house had stopped smoldering, and took me away.

"No, but I did. For you."

Oh. Shit. Shit. Shit. Shit. Oh. Holy. Fucking. Shit.

I glanced around. I could scream, but he'd only say I was crazy or something. I could run, but he'd find me. He'd slept with Sarah. God, he'd done it to get close to me. No question.

But this?

"You... what?"

"I saw the way he tried to touch you. Heard all the sick things he said he'd do. I knew what would happen if I didn't stop him because you were to be mine. Not his. He was a drunk. An asshole. No one liked him, so I finished him. He made it easy. All I had to do was light a cigarette and get the recliner to catch."

"You wanted your father dead?" I had to wonder what Ron had done to RJ.

Tears slid down my cheeks, the only outlet for my emotions.

"I wanted you and he stood in my way."

"I won't tell," I said, although that was stupid. He'd gotten away with it five years ago. Nothing I could say to anyone would change that now.

"I'll tell Dr. Wainright you didn't save my father. That you walked right past him, unconscious and helpless, and let him die. The professor won't want you then. No one will except someone who understands."

I swallowed hard, swiped my hand over my face.

"Me."

I turned and fled, sprinting past people on the path, trying to get away from RJ as fast as possible.

I wanted to go to East's, to hide at his house. To feel his arms around me again, to know I wasn't alone.

Over the weekend, I'd felt like I belonged. A part of a family.

It had been real. Too real. But it could never happen.

I couldn't give this problem to East. He had so much family shit of his own to deal with. Hell, he *fought* in underground fights to deal with his demons.

I couldn't give him mine. I already had though. I'd been selfish and thought of this complaint only from my side. What kind of trouble was East in? Would he be fired? Certainly called out by his peers.

I'd started all this with my ridiculous jealousy. If I hadn't gone to that fight, RJ never would have found me. I cared about East and this was what it gave me. A nightmare.

I got to my car, fumbled to get the key in the lock. Glancing over my shoulder, I looked for RJ. He wasn't there, but no matter how quickly I fled, I knew he'd find me.

19

EAST

THE ONE THING about the dean, she didn't spread shit. In the math department, no one looked at me funny, commented on the hearing. Nothing. Clearly, they didn't know.

I had to talk to Ella, but I didn't dare text. Didn't try calling. Wouldn't show up at her apartment because I didn't want to make it worse for her. So I went to her work all the way out by the airport and waited for her in the parking lot, just like I had before. I blocked her car in with my truck and leaned against it to wait. We were talking.

This time when she came out, she looked worn down. Broken. Fragile. Exhausted.

When she approached, she didn't stay away. Instead, she walked right into me. I hadn't expected that, but instinctively, I wrapped my arms around her, hugged her fiercely. She burst into tears.

I let her cry into my flannel as I stroked her hair, kissed the top of her head. Fuck. She was killing me. I didn't know a stronger woman, one whose drive to succeed pushed her forward. One day at a time, she worked toward her goal with a single-minded focus that kept everything else secondary. Including me. Including her emotions.

"Tell me, doll," I murmured when her sobs turned into sniffles.

She pulled back and I let her go, setting my hand on her shoulder.

"I can't. You shouldn't be here." She glanced over her shoulder. "Someone's watching."

"No one here cares about you in college," I said. Everyone heading for their cars had also finished a full shift. It was late and bitterly cold. All they wanted was to go home.

She shook her head and stepped back. Wiped her face with a mitten covered hand. "You can't be here."

"I'm going to take care of this," I vowed. I hadn't heard from Jed. Yet.

Instead of looking at me with hope, like I was her own personal superhero, she held up a hand, refused to even glance my way. As if she was blocking me out. "No. You need to stay away from me. You can't fix this. It's all my fault."

All her fault? "You've done nothing wrong, doll."

She shook her head, her eyes wide and almost pleading in the dark. "I have."

"You didn't come onto me for a better grade. Your virginity's proof that's not your M.O."

The look she gave would have withered a lesser man. "This isn't about that!"

"I know," I shouted back. It didn't matter how we met; it was that we were in this fuck-all situation together. She just didn't see it that way. Well, she would. "I said I would protect you and I will. Why won't you let me?"

"Because we can't be together. We can't be in a relationship." She looked up at me with such sadness I wanted to grab her again. She held up her hand to ward me off. Like she was tainted or dirty. She'd let me hug and comfort her, which was a sign that this wasn't over. She found safety in me. Her guard went down and she'd cried. I had to wonder when the last time was she'd done that.

Still, she was pushing me away.

"We can be in a relationship. I was wrong. I want one with you. I've never had one before because it had never been you."

Yeah, that was one fucking huge admission. But it was the truth.

She shook her head. "Go, East. You need to go."

She wasn't going to be swayed and I was only making it worse. No matter how much I hated it, I got in my truck and pulled away. I'd finally found the person I wanted to be with. My other half. The person who soothed my demons. Hell, made me forget I even had them because life wasn't so dark when I had Ella, pure brightness. I watched from the back of the lot as she pulled out, followed her at a distance until she got to her apartment. I'd take care of this. I'd take care of her. Then I'd make her mine.

20

EAST

"I EMAILED YOU," Jed said the second I answered his call. It was early and I hadn't gone to campus yet. I'd had a shower and was drinking my coffee, but this was more of a wakeup than caffeine.

I went into my home office and opened my laptop. "What's in there?" I asked, dropping into my chair and waiting for the screen to turn on.

"Ella Taynor, twenty-two, born in Missoula. Mom's listed as Eleanor Taynor. No father. Mom was called by social services several times before they ultimately took Ella away. Mom died two years later. Overdose. Ella stayed in foster care until she was eighteen."

"That's it?" I asked, entering my password.

"She was in eight foster care homes. It took time to look at all of the families. None of them are going to win any awards, but they provided stable and safe homes."

"But..." I could hear it in his voice there was more coming. I probably wasn't going to like it.

"Her last place, she was only there a few months before she turned eighteen. It had me looking into the one prior, why she left so close to aging out."

I found his email, opened the report. There were so many pages, I wasn't sure what to look at first.

"That place... well, shit. I can see why she said she wants to be a social worker."

"Jesus, Jed. Just tell me."

"Ron Silvers, the man of the house. In and out of prison for petty crimes. Including aggravated assault."

I set my coffee mug down, ran my hand through my damp hair.

"They had seventeen kids through their house over the years. All but one were female." Jed's voice tipped toward grim. He was a cool customer to begin with, but he sounded extra calm. Not good.

"It's all in there, but I'll give the highlights. Complaints to social workers came in about Ron touching them. Nothing sexual, but handsy. Verbal comments about what he was going to do with the kid. Nothing substantiated by any of them because they recanted when pressed."

"And that wasn't a red flag?"

"A fire destroyed the house. Killed Ron Silvers. Report says he was a drunk and passed out with a cigarette in his hand."

"He set his own house on fire?" I asked.

"Yes. His wife, who had to have had the shit kicked out of her to turn a blind eye to a handsy asshole for a husband, got out. So did everyone else. Ella, a younger foster girl, and the Silvers' son, RJ."

I kept scrolling through the pages. Saw a clipping of the house fire from the local newspaper.

There were more pictures. A mug shot of Ron Silvers, his wife, who looked a decade older than she should, and then–

I sat bolt upright. Stared.

"I know that guy."

"Who?" Jed asked.

"Holy shit. RJ Silvers. He was at the fight last month. The one Ella came to. He was with her. Had his arm around her shoulders. She wasn't thrilled about it. I saw it all from the ring and had to finish off my opponent to get to her. I knocked him down and carried Ella off."

"This changes things. Hang on."

I heard the shuffling of papers, silence, which I assumed was him reading either the printouts or off his computer.

"RJ stands for Ron Junior. Looking at the photos I shared, they definitely share DNA. He was eighteen at the time of the fire. Only… six months older than Ella. After the fire–Ella was immediately sent to that last foster home–he and his mom moved into a trailer on the edge of town. Bank account data in his name shows less than two hundred dollars. Tax records list minimum wage jobs, barely making enough to pay Uncle Sam."

I definitely didn't like the kid.

"Hang on," he said again.

I was impatient, trying to figure out why he was with Ella at the fights. Was it a coincidence they met there after all those years apart? She had only gone because of the conversation I'd had with Callie.

"His mother died in a trailer park fire last year. A windstorm blew an electrical line down. It arced against the wood steps."

"Let me guess, RJ was there."

"He was. Told the police that the trailer had engulfed so quickly he had to jump out his bedroom window at the back."

"It doesn't take a math genius–or two decades with the FBI–to see that one plus one might just equal a psychopath."

"Yeah. This is bad."

I didn't blame Jed. He had no involvement in any of this police work we were working through. Not the first crime, nor the second. He had the big picture here and it was easy to see.

"I doubt a fire inspector would even know to look at previous family history if all indicators of ignition were accidental," he said.

"Which means Ella lived with a murderer," I said, narrowing all the data down to one sentence.

"Tell me about your relationship," he said. We weren't giving each other pedicures while watching a Jane Austen movie. He was thinking like an investigator.

"She picked me randomly at the bar," I began. "I was only there for a quick beer after a fight. I'd decided to stop in at the last minute."

"So she didn't target you."

"No. I didn't know anything about her. She ghosted me, until the next day when I showed up to teach her stats class."

"Planned? She knew this and followed you?"

I didn't like him painting Ella to be diabolical, but I understood.

"No. No one knew. Her stats professor gave birth that night, two months early. We were scrambling to fill her classes. I was randomly assigned Ella's stats class only that morning. Even so, I can't see why she would jeopardize all she's worked for because of math elective. She's six months from graduating. You met her, she wants to be a social worker and nothing is going to steer her from that path."

"Right. So she didn't plan it. What about fight night?"

"Again, not planned." I outlined why.

"But that was where she saw RJ SIlvers."

"Yes. She came home with me after. Spent the night. After that, we didn't get together again until Thanksgiving. Oh shit..."

"What?"

"I asked her to come. She turned me down. At the last minute, she changed her mind. Texted and asked if she could go with me."

"You think because of Silvers?" Jed asked.

"We returned Saturday before dark." Jed and North had waved us off when we'd returned to town in the helicopter, so he knew that much. "The next day, she worked. I met her in the parking lot after. She wanted nothing to do with me. Told me we were done. The next morning, I got the call from the dean. I went and saw her after work last night." I didn't remember if Jed knew, so I told him about where she worked and her hours. "She'd said... oh fuck. She'd said someone was watching." I popped out of my chair like a fighter jet ejector seat. "I thought she was talking about the other workers, that it bothered her for us to be seen together. Do you think she was talking about Silvers?"

If she had been, then she was dealing with this fucker on her own. She was afraid of him and for good reason.

The line was quiet, but I knew Jed was thinking. "Let's say Silvers is behind all this. He runs into her by accident at the fights. Sees her again after all these years. The last time was when he set his father on fire because he was a dirty man with a penchant for female foster kids. She could've just disappeared again, but you told him to fuck off and stole her away. You fought. You're known there. He could ask anyone about you."

"He'd have learned I was a professor easy enough."

"Right. He tracks her down to campus, maybe he approaches her. She freaks and spends the weekend with you to get away from him. She returns. He's not done with her and lodges the complaint so she'll be kicked out of school."

"Fuck, Jed, that's messed up."

"I have a feeling we don't even have the whole picture. Call Ella. Get her to talk. Hang on." He must've put his hand over the phone because I could hear him talking but it was muffled. "North agrees," he said after a bit. "Ella needs to tell you what's going on."

I shook my head, but he couldn't see. "I can't. She won't have anything to do with me."

"The hearing is tomorrow? If it goes bad what will happen?"

"Yeah, it's at ten. Worst case? She gets kicked out of school. Loses her scholarship. Can't go to grad school. I get a slap on the wrist by the dean and a slap on the back by a few of my misogynistic peers for doing what they've always wanted. Bagging a hot coed."

"Bottom line, she didn't ask you to fix her grades." It wasn't a question.

"Hell, no. I checked. She's got a low B in the class."

"I'll work on finding more about Silvers. North says she'll have the lawyers on standby." I wasn't sure what lawyers were going to do. Nothing illegal had happened. No one was going to jail. "You work on a way to prove the only thing you two did was fall in love."

He hung up. I stared at the laptop screen. Fall in love? Had I fallen in love with Ella?

Fuck me, I had. Because saving her was more important than saving myself. She had me on her side. Her dreams were now mine and I'd see them happen. Now I knew what Jed had felt like when all that shit was coming at North over the summer. While he'd been undercover and trying to see if she had been part of Macon's underhanded and illegal deals, he'd fallen for her. There wasn't a more stubborn or brave woman than my sister, although it was looking like Ella was right there with her. Jed had literally kidnapped North and hidden her away in his off-the-grid cabin to protect her. I hadn't been able to stop him.

It wasn't a bad idea, whisking Ella away from all her dangers. Then there was South, who'd lost his shit when he found out Maisey had been keeping a lump in her breast secret. That was also life or death shit. Yeah, I got them now. I was as pussy whipped as they were and damned glad to be in the club. Except Ella's shit wasn't resolved. I had to save my woman.

Nothing would get in the way. It was time to go to work and figure this shit out.

21

ELLA

THE REVIEW MEETING was in a conference room in the administration building. I'd never been to the second floor. The table was oval and sat at least twelve. However, there were only three from the university sitting across from me. The math department dean, who I'd never met before, Dr. Ambrose, the sociology dean and an administrator from some office that oversaw ethics and other complaints. I'd never felt so alone in my life.

I wished East was beside me, to hold my hand and tell me everything was going to be okay. I hadn't seen RJ again after the confrontation outside of the sociology building. He was around. I knew it. What happened during this meeting wasn't his making, but he'd been the catalyst to bring it about. He'd want to know the outcome because me being kicked out of school was his plan. He wanted me to leave town with him. Be his.

I swallowed down bile as I thought about the idea. My palms were sweaty and I wiped them on my skirt. I'd skipped my usual jeans and sneakers for a skirt and tights. I'd spent time on my hair and makeup so I looked smart and professional. Except the meeting was about me sleeping with a professor in exchange for a good grade, which made them probably think me a whore.

"What is your relationship with Dr. Wainright?" Dr. Ambrose asked. As the head of my major's department, I'd met her at a few holiday functions. She was nice, but all cheer was absent now. She was by the books professional.

"I am not in a relationship with Dr. Wainright," I replied. Out of all the terms the dean could use, it had to be that one. I'd fought and fought with East about being with him, pushing him away even for his own good.

"That isn't what it says here," she added, glancing down at an open folder of papers in front of her.

"The question is, did I have sex with Dr. Wainright for an improved grade in the statistics class. The answer is no."

"You didn't have sex with him?" the administrator said, although I couldn't remember her name nor could I ask it now.

"Is there a rule that says a professor and a student can't have sex?" I asked. I was trying to sound calm and professional while I was losing my shit on the inside. Three years–and almost another semester–of schooling came down to a thirty minute meeting.

"It is unethical due to the power dynamics," the administrator clarified.

"Meaning the professor has the power or the student? It seems I could have him fired, and yet I haven't lodged a complaint. As far as I know, it wasn't Dr. Wainright who lodged a complaint against me."

The administrator squirmed. "Or if another student feels slighted by bias."

"Except this wasn't lodged by another student in the class either. Was it?" I knew who it was, but did they? "My grades would be exemplary if I slept my way to an A."

The door to the meeting room opened. "She's right. If I were giving a student a tit-for-tat trade, giving someone a low B isn't very equitable."

East.

"Dr. Wainright, this doesn't involve you," Dr. Ambrose said, pursing her lips.

"It does because I'm one of the accused. Please pull up Miss Taynor's grades from your pile of papers."

They looked at him, annoyed, but when he settled into a chair beside me, they knew he wasn't leaving. I looked to him. He wore jeans, but a white button up shirt and tie. Even a sport coat. He gave me his fair eyes, then winked. Beneath the table, he set his palm on my thigh.

He was here. He was here! My hero had come to save me. There wasn't a white horse, but I didn't care about fairy tales because they weren't real.

"I brought a copy if needed," he added.

The administrator shook her head as she put on her reading glasses. "That won't be necessary."

"As you can see, over the course of the semester, Miss Taynor's grades ranged from a C to the highest grade of a B+. Dr. Newburgh had her baby on October tenth. You will see from the grading system printout that Miss Taynor's overall grade at that time was an eighty-three point six. Since I took over the class, her grade has actually dropped. She now has an eighty-one point two."

East paused and ensured they were following

along. I was barely breathing. My heart was beating so hard I could barely hear over the rushing in my ears.

"I have to admit, it's good that Miss Taynor is not a math major because I'd have to advise her to seek an alternate direction. Dr. Simmons, if she were a freshman or sophomore with math aspirations, wouldn't you agree?"

East was telling me I was shitty at math. Was my inability to understand numbers going to save me from this?

"I'm sure we all have more important things to do than this meeting, so let's get to the point. You can clearly see there has been zero advantage given to Miss Taynor by way of grades. You can interview any number of the work study math tutors who worked for hours with her on her homework assignments and quiz prep. However, I'm suggesting an equitable and reasonable way to wrap this up. First off, Dr. Simmons, since you've taught statistics, please review Miss Taynor's homework assignments since I took over the class. It's all online and the work is written out, you'll clearly see what she's grasped and what she hasn't. Second, there is only one assignment left prior to finals. It can be sent to you for your review and grading, bypassing me entirely. I suggest an alternate professor proctor and grade the final exam."

The three who held my life in their hands looked between each other as if they could speak telepathically. "Very well," Dr. Simmons said. "Your suggestions are reasonable ones. Since you were only the temporary professor for the class and the grades show consistency across the semester."

I wasn't sure if I understood. She was telling me there wasn't an issue? What would have happened if I was an A+ student? Hope filled me and I glanced at East, who wrapped his knuckles on the table with one hand and gave my thigh a squeeze with the other.

"If there is any issue of ethical impropriety," he continued. "It is my fault and mine alone with regards to my... time with Miss Taynor. However it is none of your business, especially since we just ruled that the grade advantage is non-existent."

East gave them a pointed look, then stood and opened the door. I knew him and had seen him riled, seen him lose control with his opponent in the cage. Here, he was in command of himself. And the entire situation.

My meeting had been completely taken over by East. But it wasn't over. A woman and two men came in, all dressed in professional business suits. They looked stiff and like they had sticks up their butts.

"These are Miss Taynor's lawyers."

My eyes practically bugged out of my head. I had lawyers?

"They are here to discuss with you the fact that someone filed these complaints against her, someone who is not a student, but who is wanted for murder, stalking and a few other crimes."

"We don't know what you're talking about," the administrator said, looking between the three lawyers as if they might eat her.

They settled into chairs on either side of me, sitting upright and waiting, perhaps, for when it was their turn to speak.

The door opened again. Holy shit. Jed?

He took off his Stetson and nodded to the trio. "I'm Jed Barnett, head of security for Wainright Holdings but also former FBI. While I'm sure you take your ethics issues seriously, it's time to talk about something that's actually important. Miss Taynor's safety. Campus police has taken an adult male into custody outside of this building, using this trumped-up complaint and this specific meeting to lure her away from campus."

RJ had been caught? My heart was like a hummingbird in my chest. I was shaky with adrenaline and too much to keep up with.

East came over, took my hand and tugged me to

my feet. He seemed bigger now, his touch stronger. I felt weak and vulnerable because of the meeting and knowing RJ had been waiting for me outside. But with East, I felt as if I wasn't alone. "Come on, doll. Let's let these guys take care of the rest. You're always safe with me." He looked to his department dean. "I assume, Dr. Simmons, you'll be in touch with Miss Taynor about the homework assignment?"

She nodded, then swallowed hard, darting a glance at the lawyers and Jed.

East smiled almost smugly, as if content to throw some weight around. Instead of in the ring, he'd been fighting for me. He led me out of the room. I glanced over my shoulder one last time and Jed gave me a wink. The door closed and that was it.

East pulled me down the hall, but I stopped. The tug on his hand had East turning to face me. "Is RJ really caught?" I asked, petrified to hope too much. Tears filled my eyes and I blinked hard to keep them from falling. In this moment, I'd walk away from the university if I knew that I'd be forever rid of RJ.

He tucked my hair behind my ear and stepped close. There were others in the hallway, but they didn't pay us any attention.

"Yes."

I took a deep breath. "How? I mean... how did you–"

"Know about RJ?" he asked in return. His jaw clenched, although I wasn't sure if it was because he was upset about RJ or angry at me that I hadn't mentioned him.

I nodded.

"We knew he wanted you–"

I set my hand on his chest. Felt the heat of him, the firmness of his pec. "Wait. How did you know about him?"

His gaze narrowed. "Not because you told me, doll."

"We're not in a relationship so I–"

He set his hand over mine. "I'm starting to hate that word," he murmured. "That's something we need to talk about."

I wasn't sure about that, so I prompted, "RJ?"

"I had Jed look into you."

"Me?"

"You were pushing me away and not telling me shit. The perk of being a Wainright is access to anything I need."

I thought of the helicopter.

"Plus, Jed's former FBI, and easily got everything on you."

Everything?

"It included photos and one of them was of Silvers. I recognized him from the fight. Jed took it from there. Figured out he'd been following you since fight night and was the one who lodged the complaint, so then he'd be here. He's a sick fuck, so he'd want to see your face when you came out of the building. He'd want to see that he destroyed you."

God, he'd have gotten off on it.

Still, it was all so much. "Jed just... walked up to him and arrested him?"

East shrugged and led me down the hall to the steps, then out the main doors. "Pretty much, with the help of campus police." He pointed to the right and there were several officers surrounding... tears filled my eyes.

RJ was in cuffs and one of the campus police was talking with him.

Because he was creepy as fuck, he must have sensed me or something else that made my skin crawl, because he looked my way. His gaze met mine. The dark eyes narrowed and he was angry.

Yeah, I'd done this to him. No, East had. East had ensured I was safe from a creep like him. A murderer. I wouldn't cower, so I lifted my chin, glared, then turned my back.

East leaned down, set his hands on my shoulders so I couldn't look at anything but him. "It's over. He's out of your life for good."

I nodded and took a deep breath, focused on what was in front of me, not behind.

"We need to talk, doll. About everything I didn't cover." His voice was soft, almost gentle, but he wasn't going to sway on this.

I owed him everything. He'd stood up for me, had my back when no one else ever had. He might have alluded to how I wasn't skilled at math, but I could let that slide.

"Yeah."

He took my hand. "Let's go."

"Where?"

"Wherever I am, doll."

Wherever I am. That sounded about right.

22

EAST

This time when I led her into my house, I stopped in the kitchen instead of taking her to the shower. I dropped my keys on the granite counter and leaned a hip against it.

"I want to stop bringing you here after fights," I said.

She paused as she took off her coat and frowned.

"The fight at the warehouse and now at the university."

I took the jacket from her and hung it on a peg in the mudroom.

"You should give up the math department and take up English. I think that's an allegory or something."

He arched a brow. "And you should stick with sociology."

She smiled. "Agreed."

"I haven't been back," I told her. "The warehouse. It's because of you."

"Me?" she said, setting her hand on her chest.

I liked her in her skirt and sweater, the flirty hem reminding me of the dress she'd worn when we'd first met. The thick tights would make it hard to flip it up and fuck her against my counter. Hard, not impossible.

I tried to hide the tension I'd felt earlier. The frustration over the meeting, the need to have to prove ourselves. Then there was Silvers and all Jed and I had done overnight to see him finished. If what Jed believed was true–and the evidence stuck–Silvers would be going away for life. Knowing he'd be behind bars and couldn't get to Ella made me feel a hell of a lot better.

I'd agreed with Jed that I shouldn't be around when Silvers was picked up. If there was a guy I wanted to beat the shit out of–besides Macon–it was RJ Silvers. He'd said it wouldn't be good for me to do it in the middle of a busy campus, which proved Jed hadn't cared about what I did to the guy, only that I didn't have a bunch of witnesses.

So I'd gone inside, forcing myself not to scan every student I passed as I cut across campus. My job had been to clear Ella at the hearing. Jed would see her safe from Silvers and I'd ensure her dreams stayed on track. I'd do anything for her. She wouldn't believe words, but actions? She had to know how I felt about her now.

Now she was here. Having her in my house... it made it feel like a home. Like there could be something more to the place than just where I ate and slept. But we had shit to hash out. A lot of it based on the fact that she never mentioned she had a murdering psychopath after her.

"Want a drink?" I asked.

"Um, sure," she replied.

I went to the fridge, grabbed a specialty soda she'd liked the last time and handed it to her.

As she popped the top, I asked, "Did you come for Thanksgiving only to get away from Silvers?"

She swallowed hard, then wiped her mouth with the back of her free hand. "I... I did. RJ was dating my roommate, Sarah, to get close to me." She froze, her eyes widening. "Oh God, Sarah. Is she okay?"

Her words were not fucking helping. We hadn't

found that in our digging. I pulled out my cell, texted Jed about Sarah and to ensure she and the other roommates were safe. Then I put the device away.

"I'm sure she's fine, but I asked Jed to check," I told her.

She nodded. "He threatened me, said that he'd never let me go again."

I crossed my arms over my chest, trying to remain calm. The fact that he'd been that close to her–

"My roommates go home for the break and I'd have been there alone. He knew that and I was scared. I..."

"Used me to get away." Fuck, that hurt.

She took a step toward me, then stopped. Her shoulders dropped and she sighed. "I did. I know that sounds bad, but you were the first and only person I thought of to help. I... I knew I'd be safe with you, because even that night at the bar—Remember? You even asked me why I picked you."

I nodded. If I wanted to know the truth, I had to let her talk. No matter what it was.

"From the moment I saw you, I felt something." Her voice was soft, but determination lit her eyes. "Something different than I had with anyone else. I somehow knew you'd take care of me, that things would be okay. So when I freaked out, it was you I ran to."

"Why didn't you tell me about it all then? We'd have gotten Jed involved sooner. You could have come here and stayed."

She shook her head. "Because of everything that just happened with the complaint. I told you it was possible. If you hadn't helped, I'm not sure if I'd have been cleared."

"You were doing a good job of it when I came in. But I see you were right." I had to concede that. Her caution had been warranted. Of course an asshole like Silvers never came to mind, but still.

"There are hotels, other places to stay besides here. You didn't want to tell me." I held up my hand. "If you say it's because we're not in a relationship, I'll take you over my knee and I'll make you sure you don't like it. This time."

She bit her lip, looked away. Tears filled her eyes and with a shaky hand, she brushed them away as they slid down her cheeks. I wanted to go to her and hug her, to take even this pain from her. I couldn't. She had to tell me everything.

"You said Jed dug into my past. You know about RJ, so you know about his father, Ron."

I nodded.

Her voice grew softer and she wrapped her arms around herself.

"Fuck this," I grumbled.

Yeah, I couldn't not touch her. In two steps I had an arm wrapped around her and led her into my great room and settled on the couch, tugging her onto my lap.

"East," she gasped, then wiggled to get settled.

Maybe this was a bad mistake because my dick perked up at the feel of her lush curves pressed against it. I couldn't help but touch her and ran a hand down her back. My dick was going to have to wait.

"Go on," I prompted.

"He was... an asshole."

I couldn't help but smile at that, then it slipped because she'd been living, as a kid, with an asshole. I knew exactly what that was like.

"He watched me. Cornered me. Told me that he wanted to touch me. That was for a few months. Then he told me he was *going* to touch me. I jumped at every sound, ensured I was always in a room with another person. Showered at school. Besides being a perv, he was mean. Belligerent, especially when he drank, which was all the time. He hit his wife to keep her in line. I think he did it enough so that she would be too scared of him to complain to anyone about messing with the foster kids."

I pulled her close, tucked her head under my chin and wrapped my arms around her. The house was quiet except for her words. She shivered and I knew it wasn't from being cold.

I kissed her brow and felt how silky soft she was. Her scent swirled around me. Knowing she was in my hold, safe and protected was the best feeling in the world.

"One night, the smoke alarms went off. The others must have gone down the back stairs, but I went the other way. I have no idea why. I don't even remember thinking about it. I found Ron passed out in his recliner, which was on fire. It had spread around the room. I remember the liquor bottle on the tray table beside him. It was... God, awful. I could have saved him. I could have dragged him out by his feet."

But she didn't. "The place was on fire, doll."

"But I didn't help him. I didn't want him to live because I knew I'd be moved to another foster home, but I was close to eighteen and I was going to age out. Some other girl would have been next."

"He deserved to die," I said through gritted teeth. "I'd have killed him for you."

She set her hand on my arm. “You’d have done a good job, too.”

I laughed, feeling lighter. It was as if all the years of using my knuckles had been in readiness for her, if I’d only known she existed.

“This is why you didn’t want to tell me about Silvers?”

She nodded against my chest. Her hand settled on mine and I tangled my fingers with hers. “I didn’t know this then, but RJ knew I hadn’t saved his father. When I saw him again at the fight–it was the first time since that night–he was the key to my past, the one I thought I’d left behind.”

I turned her so I could meet her eyes. She couldn’t hide now that she told me. Settling her so her knees were on either side of my hips, she straddled me. I even tipped her chin up. “Doll, RJ set the fire.”

“I know,” she replied. “He told me the other day. Looking back, he must’ve used the liquor to make the fire spread. Because if it had been Ron’s cigarette, he would have burned too. And first.”

She shivered again.

“When he admitted it, it all became so much worse.”

“His mother died in a trailer home fire. Jed thinks he set it.”

She gasped and her thighs clenched against me. "Oh my God."

"You didn't kill Ron Silvers, doll." She glanced away and I tipped her chin back. "Even if you left him like you thought, good riddance."

Her blinking eyes told me I'd confused her.

"I'm the last person who'd ever think bad of you for something like that."

"I figured you'd run," she admitted.

I gave her a squeeze. "You see me running? I told you I took up fighting to deal with my anger toward Macon. I'd have killed him if I could have gotten away with it. So I kept fighting because that was how I dealt with him and survived. I kept right on doing it until that night. The night that things came together for me and everything went to shit for you."

"How did it come together?" she asked.

"Fight night. You here in my house with me. What we did... Fuck, doll. I knew at the bar I was in trouble. We agreed to no strings and I was fine with that. No strings but I wasn't letting you go. Yeah, that makes no fucking sense, does it?"

I ran a hand over my hair, thinking back and realizing how stupid I'd been.

"I've gone to the gym. Sparred. But no competitions, none at the warehouse. I have something to fight for now, something different than my anger at Macon."

"What's that?" Her green eyes met mine, full of hope.

"Us. You and me. Jed told me I loved you. Yeah, that sounds stupid, but what the hell did I know? But it's true. I do. I've never said it to anyone before, not even my siblings."

I couldn't help but kiss her. Gentle, sweet and soft. My dick stirred, but it wasn't time to fuck. I was content to have her on my lap. Finally, *finally* pulling our heads out of our asses.

"I don't know how to love," she admitted. "I have no role models. No idea what I'm doing."

"You think I do?" I countered.

"You've got family."

"You do too now. Just because–"

She set her palm over my mouth to shut me up.

"I didn't realize when you care about someone, it's out of your control," she admitted. "It's not something you can plan or try to handle how you feel. I thought if we set boundaries and both agreed that this wasn't anything other than sex, then that's what it would be."

I lowered her hand. "We sure were stupid."

She smiled and cupped my cheek.

"I have no clue what I'm doing, East. None. I've

had one focus for so long, I didn't even know there was anything else. Then when you came along, I was so scared I'd lose my dream. But... I chose you at the bar. I gave you my panties in the copy room."

My dick perked up at that memory.

"I turned to you when I was scared. I crave you. Miss you. Need you. Not to just to protect me, but because–"

"You complete me," I told her.

She gave me a funny look, not what I was expecting to such an admission.

"Isn't that a line in some movie?"

I thought for a moment. "I have no fucking clue. I'm the math nerd, remember?"

"You're my hero," she whispered.

"Your fairy tale prince? Because if so, you're Cinderella."

She frowned. "I'll explain later."

I stroked her hair, her arms, her sides. "I want a relationship with you. I want to be with you, only you. I want to be your boyfriend or whatever label you want to give me as long as you're in my bed every night and wake up next to me every morning."

"Yes," she replied. "I want a relationship with you, too."

I cupped her ass and stood, keeping her in my

arms. Her ankles hooked behind my back as I carried her into my bedroom.

23

ELLA

I COULDN'T BELIEVE IT. East loved me. Me! I wasn't completely out of trouble with the university, but I'd be supervised by the department dean. Unless I got an A+ on my last assignment and final, I'd be in the clear. Not that there was any chance of that. I'd let East be the math genius.

Then there was RJ. He–

East lowered me to his bed and began kissing down my neck. RJ was in jail and wasn't getting out anytime soon. I was sure I'd have to make a statement at some point. I'd have to talk with Sarah and explain. All of that could wait.

East was making me forget about everything but him.

The weight of him. His heat. His scent. His touch.

I craved him and needed him and loved him and–

I wanted everything with him. It seemed it was possible.

"I can feel you thinking. Clearly, I'm not doing something right," East murmured against my skin.

I hooked my hand behind his neck, looked up in his pale eyes.

"You're perfect."

He huffed out a laugh.

"For me you are," I countered.

His smile softened and his gaze heated.

"You're the only one I care about," he murmured.

"East," I breathed and pulled him down for a kiss. He let me as there was no way I'd be able to manhandle him otherwise.

"You're wearing way too many clothes." He sat back on his heels and let his hands roam. "I hate winter outfits." My skirt got pushed up. "Tights should be banned."

I helped him push them down my hips and wriggle them lower.

He took them and my shoes at the same time, dropped them on the floor.

Now my skirt was up around my waist.

"Panties should be banned too."

"You can't keep taking them," I countered when he hooked his fingers in the sides and worked them off.

"You'll be living here, so I'll only be ensuring they remain in your drawer."

"I am not going commando at the distribution center."

He lowered himself between my thighs, parted my knees wider so he could fit. "You want to work there, doll?"

"No, but it pays the bills."

"You live here, you have no rent."

I pushed up onto my elbows. "We're talking about this now, with you..." I twirled my finger between us. "There?"

He grinned mischievously.

"You agree to quit, I lick your pussy."

It was my turn to laugh. "East, I can't–"

"You love me?" he asked seriously.

"Yes." My answer was immediate and the way his eyes softened made me so happy.

"Then stop working there. Stop killing yourself for your dream. You might still want to be a social worker, but you've got other wants now too."

He was right. I relied on East already for safety and protection, I should let him help me other ways too.

"I can't reciprocate. I never will."

His gaze lowered to my pussy and his hands shifted to cup my ass and part me. "I can think of ways you can reciprocate."

He licked me and I moaned. My fingers went to his hair and tangled.

"This is exactly how we got into trouble in the first place. Rec–ipro–cation." I was gasping by the time I was done.

"I love you, you love me. That's the beginning and end of it."

He didn't say more, only slipped a finger inside and sucked on my clit. I couldn't argue if I tried. *He* was trying to make me forget everything but his name and that it was him and only him who could make me complete.

I came on a clench and a scream. Only when I was slumped on the bed, sweaty and replete did he stand and wipe his mouth with the back of his hand. He stripped and grabbed a condom from the drawer.

I watched him the whole time and reveled that this guy was mine. He tugged me to the edge of the bed, hooked the back of my knees so he was standing on the floor and aligned at my entrance. I hooked my ankles about his waist, and he dropped his hands on either side of my head. All I could see was him. The dark hair, the love and heat and need in his eyes. The soft turn of his lips. The rugged jaw.

Him. East Wainright.

Mine.

He thrust deep and I knew I was complete.

Ready for more Billionaire Ranch?

Turn to West now!

TURNED OUT, Rory Sullivan, the New York lawyer who'd been waiting at the airport, was not a guy. And she had the prettiest nipples I'd ever seen. How the hell did I know that? Because I was eyeing them, watching as they hardened in the cool air of her hotel room.

"You going to look or are you going to touch?" she asked, reaching up and taking off my Stetson. She tossed it somewhere behind me as I continued to take in those hard tips.

Fuck if that ballsy question didn't make my dick hard. *Harder.*

I had one hand braced on the door above her head. I was close, but not touching. We hadn't made it any further into the room before I spun her to face the door, slid the zipper down the back of her high-powered dress and pushed it down to her hips. Next went the catch on her bra and when I turned her back around, it fell right off.

She was a tiny thing and my head was tilted down to take her all in, but I lifted my gaze from her spectacular rack to her green eyes.

"You going to stop with the sass or am I going to have to make you?" I asked.

Her eyes flared with a mixture of determination, fury and need at my question.

This hate/fuck banter had been going on since baggage claim. She'd come to Montana a day early for a meeting at Wainright Holdings but had decided a ride on a cowboy's dick was a way to kick the trip off.

I was more than happy to oblige, as long as it was mine she was climbing on.

I'd figured her out pretty quickly. Walking into the baggage area I'd found the New Yorker my sister, North, asked me to collect and entertain. Except she hadn't been a guy. *She'd* been in a slim cut dress that screamed big city. It had a conservative cut meant for a Connecticut country club filled with stodgy rich folk, except it showed off every curve of her pint-sized body. If that wasn't enough, she wore a pair of ruthless heels that did plenty for her legs. It had been the phone connected to her head like a teenager and the way her toe tapped on the industrial carpet that clinched my thoughts about her.

Rory Sullivan, the sexy as fuck power broker, was a wound tight, sexy siren who'd made my dick hard from across the luggage conveyor belt. I'd instantly wanted to fuck the high-maintenance, East coast workaholic, who, by the half of the conversation I'd been able to overhear, probably wore a string of weak men's balls as a necklace.

Maybe that had been it, her *I'm in fucking charge* attitude that was so out of place here in Big Sky country. I wanted to bend her to my will. Get her on her knees. Fuck that priss right out of her. Make her forget the names of her clients as well as her own.

To *rule* her world.

I'd gone to the airport in the first place because my sister had discovered I was in town to do my monthly big-box store shopping and had asked. I spent my days in the saddle and no doubt she wanted me to have a conversation with a real person instead of a horse. She was worried about me now that she—a ball buster herself—had found Jed Barnett.

North didn't have to worry. Fuck, no. I could deal with people when I wanted. One sexy one in particular, especially naked.

I doubted North envisioned this kind of *Welcome to Montana* from me, but she sure as shit couldn't complain I wasn't being attentive. I'd headed us toward my favorite burger restaurant, intending to feed Rory dinner and drop her off at her hotel. Instead, she'd said she wanted a different kind of meat... no, she hadn't said that exactly. But something else just as bold that'd had me turning my truck toward her hotel and instead of leaving her at the entrance, escorted her to her room.

And out of her bra.

Rory's small hands went to my belt buckle as she eyed me. Tipped her chin up when she reached in and—

I hissed at the aggressive tug. "You might have your hand around my dick," I told her, leaning down to kiss those sassy lips. She moaned and I took the kiss deep. I tangled my fingers in her long hair. Pulled a little when she gave me a rough stroke. "But if you think you're in charge…"

I couldn't say much more than that, because *fuck me* her hand felt good. Her grip was firm as it slid up and down the shaft. The swipe of her thumb over the tip was like heaven. I was going to come like a guy who hadn't fucked in a while.

I'd assumed I was too old for the stranger-fucking routine, but she'd changed my mind. I *was* content about this one-off. I didn't do more, especially with a woman from the East coast. I'd dated—and fallen for—one in college, wanted more and gotten burned. Not fucking happening again.

"You sure about that?" she replied, sounding pretty happy with bringing a six-four man to his knees.

Because I did just that, dropped to my knees on the rug in front of her, tugged the dress down her hips and it pooled around her ankles. She kicked it free and there she was, a little firecracker in ruthless stilettos and a black lace thong.

The corner of my mouth tipped up. "That wet spot makes me feel pretty confident."

I ran a knuckle over the damp gusset and she sucked in a breath.

She was so fucking pretty. Flushed and silky soft, sweet scented and… I slid that scrap of fabric to the side, leaned in and licked up her seam. Yeah, she tasted sweet too.

"I'm always in charge," she breathed, then gave a little whimper.

"Why are you here, half pint?" I wanted to see how long she could hold a conversation while I was licking her pussy.

"Montana? Or with you?"

"Both."

"I close this deal, I make partner. As for you—" She actually shrugged. "—you're hot and you're probably better than the vibrator I've got in my suitcase."

My dick punched against my jeans at the thought of her in bed, legs parted and working herself with vibrating silicone. I pushed aside the thoughts of her ruthless focus on the corner office.

"Something this pretty needs more than hardware," I said, then licked her again. "Montana's a little out of your comfort zone. No skyscrapers or weak men to crush beneath those heels. So you want to feel back in charge, getting me to come to your room. Use me for your orgasms."

Her eyes flared and she blushed.

Her clit was swollen and shiny and I ran the tip of my tongue around it.

"I'm fine with the last. Hell, I'm on my knees. But I

run this show." I screwed a finger into her dripping pussy. Fuck, she was tight.

"Weston," she breathed.

If she didn't believe me, I was going to prove it to her.

Turn to West now!

BONUS CONTENT

Guess what? I've got some bonus content for you! Sign up for my mailing list. There will be special bonus content for some of my books, just for my subscribers. Signing up will let you hear about my next release as soon as it is out, too (and you get a free book...wow!)

As always...thanks for loving my books and the wild ride!

JOIN THE WAGON TRAIN!

If you're on Facebook, please join my closed group, the Wagon Train! Don't miss out on the giveaways and hot cowboys!

https://www.facebook.com/groups/vanessavalewagontrain/

GET A FREE BOOK!

Join my mailing list to be the first to know of new releases, free books, special prices and other author giveaways.

http://freeromanceread.com

ALSO BY VANESSA VALE

For the most up-to-date listing of my books:

vanessavalebooks.com

On A Manhunt

Man Hunt

Man Candy

Man Cave

Man Splain

Man Scape

Man Handle

Man Spread

The Billion Heirs

Scarred

Flawed

Broken

Alpha Mountain

Hero

Rebel

Warrior

Billionaire Ranch

North

South

East

West

Bachelor Auction

Teach Me The Ropes

Hand Me The Reins

Back In The Saddle

Wolf Ranch

Rough

Wild

Feral

Savage

Fierce

Ruthless

Two Marks

Untamed

Tempted

Desired

Enticed

More Than A Cowboy

Strong & Steady

Rough & Ready

Wild Mountain Men

Mountain Darkness

Mountain Delights

Mountain Desire

Mountain Danger

Grade-A Beefcakes

Sir Loin of Beef

T-Bone

Tri-Tip

Porterhouse

Skirt Steak

Small Town Romance

Montana Fire

Montana Ice

Montana Heat

Montana Wild

Montana Mine

Steele Ranch

Spurred

Wrangled

Tangled

Hitched

Lassoed

Bridgewater County

Ride Me Dirty

Claim Me Hard

Take Me Fast

Hold Me Close

Make Me Yours

Kiss Me Crazy

Mail Order Bride of Slate Springs

A Wanton Woman

A Wild Woman

A Wicked Woman

Bridgewater Ménage

Their Runaway Bride

Their Kidnapped Bride

Their Wayward Bride

Their Captivated Bride

Their Treasured Bride

Their Christmas Bride

Their Reluctant Bride

Their Stolen Bride

Their Brazen Bride

Their Rebellious Bride

Their Reckless Bride

Bridgewater Brides World

Lenox Ranch Cowboys

Cowboys & Kisses

Spurs & Satin

Reins & Ribbons

Brands & Bows

Lassos & Lace

Montana Men

The Lawman

The Cowboy

The Outlaw

Standalones

Relentless

All Mine & Mine To Take

Bride Pact

Rough Love

Twice As Delicious

Flirting With The Law

Mistletoe Marriage

Man Candy - A Coloring Book

ABOUT VANESSA VALE

A USA Today bestseller, Vanessa Vale writes tempting romance with unapologetic bad boys who don't just fall in love, they fall hard. Her books have sold over one million copies. She lives in the American West where she's always finding inspiration for her next story.

vanessavaleauthor.com

facebook.com/vanessavaleauthor
instagram.com/vanessa_vale_author
amazon.com/author/vanessavale
bookbub.com/profile/vanessa-vale
tiktok.com/@vanessavaleauthor

Made in the USA
Columbia, SC
14 January 2025

51791901R00143